THE GIFT

Molly Rose Series
Book
1

LAURA BUSHNELL

Editing and cover design by Joy Noe.

FIRST EDITION

Library of Congress Control Number: 2014912561
ISBN: 978-0-9711828-3-7

For you

CHAPTER ONE

Christmas is difficult for me. Well, difficult is the wrong word—more like fucking depressing. Excuse my French. My mother, Margaret St. Claire-Johnson, moved to Budapest three years ago. Her monthly calls were always the same. She would start with the weather, move on to her sister, my Aunt Sally and then take that inevitable leap into my personal life, which always led to the main reason for the call: Why wasn't I married?

"You are so pretty and smart," she would begin, "you should be married."

Then the advice would come, like a steamroller. "You should lose a few pounds, Molly. You really should join a dating site. Here's what you should write in your profile… and make sure to use a photo of your left side—it is your most flattering." One of her all-time gems was, "Think about freezing your eggs as soon as possible."

I listened to her words, hearing only *grandbaby, grandbaby, grandbaby,* like Morse code beneath her talk. My mother was obsessed. Every phone call left me feeling like a complete failure.

I was not the only one depressed. Several of my

good friends had lost their jobs and others were on the latest form of Prozac. My coping mechanism was junk food. Thanks to candy bars, cookies and ice cream I was carrying around at least twenty extra pounds. I lacked the discipline to stick with a diet and besides, who had time to exercise? Working in the bowels of the entertainment industry made it hard to lose weight. Long hours and high stress made junk food my constant companion.

Christmas Eve morning I woke up with a high fever and cough. Spoonfuls of codeine-laced cough syrup along with two aspirin put me right back to sleep. I jerked awake out of a dream, confused for a moment as to where I was. The last of the light was draining from the horizon. Christmas Eve in Los Angeles. No plans. No tree. No parties. No presents. I sat for a long while on the edge of my bed, staring into the blue-black outside, wondering how I could create my own holiday. I desperately needed to find the feeling and spirit of Christmas.

After squeezing myself into a red sweater dress, I slipped on some knee-length black boots and took the chilly walk to the parking lot. Sliding onto the cold seat of my hatchback I realized I had no idea where I was going. Why not go to church? Having grown up without religion, I had never been to church. The idea of it felt exciting to me. I did a quick search on my phone for churches in West Hollywood. There were quite a few options, so I decided to do some drive-bys, secretly hoping that someone would see me, pull me into their warm cozy church and maybe even adopt me.

The First Baptist Church must have had their service early as it was closed up tight. The Church of Religious Science was too far away, so I decided on the Catholic church off Holloway Drive. St. Victor's was a pretty church and there was a parking spot in front. I had this thing about parking spaces. If I wanted to go somewhere and was questioning whether or not I really needed to go, I would play the "parking game". It was a good sign to find the perfect spot.

St. Victor's welcomed me with that perfect spot, so I parked and went inside. No one seemed to notice me as I sat in the very back pew. Seeing all of the families sitting around me, I felt the melancholy creeping back in. I have to admit the harmonies of the children's choir singing "Silent Night" felt as though they were moving into my heart, but even that wasn't enough to get me out of my funk. I couldn't even bring myself to sing along and I had always loved that song.

I was busy feeling sorry for myself. We've all done it. Thirty-eight years old, no family to spend the holidays with and I barely had a boyfriend. He didn't even stay in town for the holidays. Mac chose to take an extra assignment with his magazine so that he would not have to deal with my "poor me" attitude. Lately my moods had been driving him away. An unfortunate downward spiral, the more I needed the more he retreated. The more he retreated, the more I needed. So when he left I tried to play it cool. I wrapped up all my emotions in a Christmas box, bow and all, and hid them from him.

All of the incense mixed with the cough syrup must have made me a bit high, because I started laughing to myself halfway through the service. The Bishop, wearing his long dress and high hat, was speaking in a language I couldn't understand. It hit me as hilarious that all these holy men were wearing dresses, while all I could think about was getting home to put on a pair of jeans. I clapped my hand over my mouth and ducked out between songs.

On the way home I had to pee so badly that I desperately looked for somewhere to stop. When a spot opened up in front of Southern Comfort, a small antique store on Melrose Avenue, I parked my car and jumped out. Thank God the light was on. When I walked through the front door, a string of bells chimed my arrival and then I heard a woman whisper my name.

"Molly."

Or at least I thought I did. The voice seemed to come from nowhere. Maybe I actually was high. I could still taste the incense in my throat.

The young man at the cash register seemed to recognize the urgent look on my face and extended his index finger towards a door with a woman's silhouette. I smiled quickly and rushed through it. A book, *The Art of the Handwritten Note, A Guide to Reclaiming Civilized Communication,* was sitting on the table near the toilet, so I randomly opened a page as I sat relieving myself. Finding no toilet paper anywhere, I tore out the page that read: *The handwritten note's rarity heightens its appeal.* Of course it was rare, most people sent texts or emails. Well, all except my mom, who didn't invite her only child to Budapest for Christmas.

It would never have occurred to Mom that I might be lonely during the holidays, she was absorbed in her new life. Nothing new, as she had been absent most of my life. Something or someone else had always been more important. Despite it all, I really loved her. I longed for more of a relationship with her but was at a loss as to how to make it happen. I felt sad as I looked at my image in the mirror above the sink. Long, dark hair unlike my mom's auburn, but her intense blue eyes were staring back at me. We even shared the same small beauty mark on our necks.

"Pull yourself together," I whispered softly to my image in the mirror.

I started to walk out of the shop but heard my name again. Turning, I found myself in front of an old leaded glass cabinet and felt a cold chill run down my body. Again, I heard my name being called. Were there hidden speakers somewhere? I looked inside the cabinet the voice seemed to be coming from, but the only item in the cabinet was a small brass container with colored stones. It seemed to be glowing as if the voice was attached to it. I felt like it was beckoning me to open the cabinet door and pick it up, so I did. I was mesmerized.

"I love you."

The voice scared the crap out of me! Nearly dropping the container, I caught it like a well-trained juggler. To shake off my delirium, I took a deep breath. Then I heard it again, clear as the bells on the door.

"Take me home. I love you. I will help you."

I don't now know to explain it. It sounds ridiculous to my own ears. And, I would not expect you to believe me, because if someone had told me the same story I would have said, "Oh bull," or if I were being polite I would say, "uh huh," and then quickly change the subject. But, it was as if I had met an old friend. I felt a burning in my chest. The room blurred and all I could see was the little container at the center of my vision. I never wanted to let it go. I cradled it and turned it over. There on its belly was a sticker that read *185 francs*.

Francs? I worried that it was actually 185 dollars. No way could I afford that. But something held me in place.

"Excuse me, how much is this little jeweled thing?" I honestly did not have a clue as to what it was, just that it loved me.

"Ahh… the relic," the young man answered as he came around from behind the counter.

"Relic?"

"Yes, it has a bone of Saint Anne inside. See the wax seal?"

He gently pried the brass cover from the back of the box to reveal a thumbprint-sized dab of red wax, imprinted with words and symbols I couldn't read. There were fine red strings embedded in the wax, extending in four directions to the edges of the back face of the container, tying the contents in. The flat wax circle and tiny strings looked like a stylized sun with four rays reaching out towards the four directions.

I stared into the wax and its miniscule hieroglyphics.

"Approved... what does that mean?"

For a moment I had the urge to step away and see if Saint Anne would talk to me, see if the voice belonged to this bone. The young man stood looking at me with a slightly bored expression.

"This seal means it has been approved by a Cardinal. Since the early days of the church, the remains of a saint or holy person were called relics, from the Latin *reliquiae*, meaning remains. Christians and non-Christians alike practice the veneration of relics," he proudly declared.

"How much is it? There's a tag that says 185 francs, and francs are not legal tender anymore, what with the euro."

The clerk frowned.

"Oh, that tag is probably old. I'm not sure about the price. This is my Auntie's shop and she is away for the holidays. Let me see if I can find the paperwork."

He excused himself into a back room for a moment and returned with a worn yellow file.

"Ah yes, here it is," he showed me the words as he read. "Jeweled theca with a first class relic of St. Anne, mother of the Virgin Mary. No written Authentic available. No charge. It has an asterisk next to it, but I have no clue what my Auntie wanted to accomplish with that. But it does say no charge."

"What do you mean, no charge? That can't be right." I was dumbfounded.

"My Auntie knows her business. She has it listed as a no charge, so that means it's a gift for you. Merry Christmas."

Smiling, he made his way back to his post behind the counter.

"Thank you. Merry Christmas to you too."

I drove home slowly, floating inside some kind of awed hush, unable to understand what had just happened. It was late at night, but the space of my hatchback seemed light-filled, bright as a lantern bobbing down a dark river. The box was nestled like a little passenger on the seat beside me, and for the first time in years I did not feel alone. I almost heard a purr, or felt one. I turned on some Christmas music in the car and actually sang "Little Drummer Boy" on the way home. I felt chosen, lucky and loved, precious and protected. It was the way I used to feel when my grandmother scooped me into her arms and held on to me real tight, or when she gave me a slice of homemade bread with fresh churned butter and sugar sprinkled all over the top.

Once I got home I made a place for her on my desk. I didn't think of her as a box or a bone. I felt St. Anne there, the little vessel was like a pulsing heart. I felt bonded to it. Grateful. I felt love.

With St. Anne in sight near my computer, I typed in a search for "relic" and found over two million results. After going through the first ten sites I began to understand that relics or the "veneration of relics" as the clerk had said, was by no means restricted to the Catholic religion rather, a primitive instinct with origins that predated Christianity.

It made sense. I felt connected by the little box on my desk to a lost time. A time when the earth was full of spirits and the living could call on them for wisdom as readily as they might call on a neighbor for some salt.

I felt my heart swell again towards her.

As I sat there, I began to feel embarrassed that I did not trust the authenticity of this little gal. I lit a candle next to her and could have sworn I heard a sigh.

A couple of days later, I caught my reflection in the mirror as I was heading towards some plants in my living room with a pitcher of water, and almost didn't recognize myself. I walked a little taller. My spine was straight and my neck was long. I kept St. Anne on the table next to my bed and I began to talk to her, although I had not heard anything since the little sigh. And that could have been the wind.

At first I just found myself murmuring a small "goodnight" when I cozied into the pillows and prepared to sleep. Then, she was the first person I greeted in the morning when I woke up. Soon I was talking to her all the time, whether she could hear me or not.

I told her my deepest miseries and my most trivial frustrations. I told her about my unhappiness at work, my lack of clarity about my purpose in life, the futility of romance and how much it annoyed me when the neighbors didn't clean up after their dogs. I shared my dreams of living a life helping others, of getting married and having a family and of traveling the world.

A month went by and I never stopped talking. Each day brought a buoyancy I hadn't felt since childhood. I started buying candles every week, like presents for a sweetheart. If I found an especially beautiful one, I would rush home to light it and share it with St. Anne. I wanted to please her and nourish her.

The thought occurred to me that I was losing my mind. Then just as quickly, I decided I didn't care. I was happy, and what did I really have to lose? Mac had been in and out of town and it didn't really faze me. He seemed insubstantial and distant—much further away than St. Anne, even when he was standing in the middle of my living room. I wanted to share St. Anne with Mac, but I didn't know how to begin. We had dated for nearly a year but there were many conversations that we just never had. If I shared my real self, I had this sneaky suspicion he would leave me for good.

My best friend Olivia came from Laguna Beach to visit. She was wearing a huge diamond engagement ring. Ever since we met in grade school, Olivia always had the same sparkly taste. Now she'd met a man who just happened to have a zillion dollars. Leave it to Olivia, she knew how to love.

We sat down to chat about the upcoming wedding—colors, patterns and themes and I had an urge to give her something, some special token of love. But what do you give the woman who has everything?

Just as I was trying to come up with an idea, Olivia pointed to St. Anne.

"What is that?" she chirped. I looked over at my relic and heard Olivia's voice again, but Olivia wasn't speaking. In my mind I heard her say, *I want that.*

And immediately after that, I heard the relic speak for the first time since the antique store. The voice was just a whisper.

"I want to be with her."

My heart stopped. I felt a deep sadness and then a rush of anger. My St. Anne. My precious friend. I wanted to snap at both of them. Where was this coming from? I took a deep breath and caught myself. I mean, this was a saint—the Virgin Mary's mother, for God's sake!

Next I heard Olivia say, "I want that."

Later, she would insist that she never said *I want that*, but rather said, *I like that*. It didn't matter, there was nothing I could do but give her what she wanted. It was the best I had and she was getting married. I smiled and handed it to her, holding back tears.

I was back to nothing. If I had done the right thing, why did I feel such a huge hole in my apartment... in my heart? I didn't know a little thing could take up so much space. There was only one thing I could think of to do.

Go back to the shop.

Maybe there was another one. Maybe I could find

my saint. One that would remain faithful to me.

CHAPTER TWO

I pushed the door open and heard the familiar tinkle of bells, but nothing more. The shop was quiet. An older woman with sky-high ultra-blonde hair wearing a soft pink Chanel suit was standing at the cash register making a martini. Southern Comfort was crowded with objects and very dusty, but the woman was perfectly neat. Her lips had been painted carefully and her movements were precise as she splashed some vermouth into a glass.

"Missy, do you like gin or would you prefer vodka? Gin martinis are much more elegant but whatever you prefer, darlin'."

I chuckled at the mention of cocktail hour. It was only 11 a.m.

"No, thank you."

The woman barely looked up from her work.

"No? Well my Lordy aren't you a little tight this mornin'? All the more reason you should join me in a little celebration."

"What are you celebrating?"

"Well this glorious day. The sun is shining, darlin'," she drawled.

I shook my head and smiled. "This is Los Angeles,

Nothing

the sun is always shining."

"Of course, honey, and what's your name? I'm Penny Anne Saylor, Proprietor."

"Molly Rose."

"Good Lord what a delightful, and might I add, fragrant name. And what brings you here on such a beautiful day?" she purred.

"I am the person who—I was given the gift, the St. Anne relic." I fidgeted slightly at the counter.

"Well it took you long enough to come get her. I thought you would have come years ago. I waited and waited to see who that little treasure was meant for."

Penny Anne was fascinating. I couldn't stop looking at her, or wanting to hear what she would say next.

"Really? How long did you know her—I mean have it?" I corrected myself.

Penny Anne twirled a frilled toothpick in her manicured fingers and gazed into the space above my head.

"While visiting the lovely city of Paris, France almost ten years ago with my third husband, Richard... oh, he was a handsome man... he loved to go to France so I'd pick up a few antiques for my business in Savannah. I found a beautiful Tiffany lampshade but the woman insisted that I also take the relic and the deck of cards that came with it. I swear she was a gypsy, that woman. She told me to give them to the first person who really wanted them. It's a mystery to me. And now it's yours. When I came back from Paris I put the relic out on the counter every day and do you know, not one person asked about it or even seemed to see it? Over the years it got moved all over tarnation. When I moved here with my fourth husband, Arnold, I had really forgotten about it till my nephew, Jimmy told me about it leavin'. I felt a great relief as if I had completed my mission. Now, Sweetie, are you ready for that martini?"

I stood staring at the woman in the pink suit and

shellacked blonde hair, dazed and enchanted. "Yes, Mrs. Saylor. I think I am."

"Just call me Penny Anne. And may I call you Molly? Oh this martini is a bit of heaven. I feel so much better already, darlin'."

"Cheers!" she exclaimed as she handed me the ice-cold perfect martini and extended her own for a toast.

"Penny Anne, you mentioned a deck of cards. Do you still have them?"

"Well you bet your life I do, dear. That's why I wondered why it had taken you so long to come back in."

"I didn't know there were cards too. I just wanted to see if you had another relic. St. Anne has already moved on to someone else."

"Oh my, that St. Anne is finicky, isn't she? Give me one little second and I'll run to the back and get you the rest of your gift. It is such a beautiful day today. Oh, I knew it was a special day. Hurry up now and drink that martini so I can make us up another batch. The second one is always better!"

Alone at the counter I took another sip of the martini. Okay, Molly, it's 11:45 a.m. on a Saturday and you are already intoxicated. I glanced aimlessly over papers and baubles, the walls plastered with antique frames and prints, feeling a bit guilty about using the page from her book as toilet paper. Should I tell her?

Penny Anne returned from the back carrying a small green cardboard box, her eyes twinkling. I didn't have a chance to plead guilty. She giggled and took another gulp of martini, forgetting the box in her hand for a moment as she recalled her life in Savannah... the humid green heat and draping Spanish Moss, the smell of honeysuckle on the night breeze. She missed the South.

As she talked and flung her arms wide to illustrate the grace of the trees and the whitewashed architecture, my eyes followed the small deck of cards captive in her fist, while she made circles and dips in the air. It made me dizzy, and I realized the martini had me swimming. I set my glass down carefully on the counter.

"Penny Anne, I must go. May I pay you for the cards?"

"Heavens no! They're part of the gift."

Too woozy to argue, I thanked her and exited the shop, blinded briefly by the shock of sun. Still blinking the light away, I found a parking ticket on my car. Now I felt like I needed a designated driver for a trip to an antique shop. Or a chaperone. Where was St. Anne when I needed her? In my mind's eye I saw her living the life of luxury at Olivia's estate. Lying on a silk chaise sipping champagne, talking away to Olivia. I'd never felt jealous of Olivia before despite her college degrees and relative success compared to mine. But now I felt a fleeting jealousy, a hollowness, and loneliness. I remembered the box in my hand and gripped it tightly. I had come for a saint but I had found something else.

When I arrived home, I opened the green box and found a miniature deck of cards. On each card was a drawing of an ornate old-fashioned key. Pink lotus flowers swirled around the edges. I looked at the cards and turned one over: *You must shortly decide a matter of much importance.* As I continued leafing through the little fortune cards, a yellowed note dropped out and fluttered to the floor. It was tissue thin and handwritten:

To the occult student who has found
this note:
I beg of you to help me. I was given
a vision as a young girl to find seven
sacred objects and bring them together
with seven women. Henry feels this is
crucial for the changes the earth is
making. We are moving into a new age.
An age of peace and enlightenment —
the return of the feminine. You will be
guided every step of the way but it
will require a sacrifice at times. If
each step were not so reinforced it
would be impossible. I started the
journey and I leave its completion to
you. You have been chosen. There are
seven saints for seven sins.

Фиолетовый крест правит вечно.
Запланировано было всё, время и
место. Бог - Роза.

Helena 1890 London.

●

My heart began to palpitate and for a few minutes I
thought I would faint. Occult student? I knew nothing
about the occult. I scanned the note with the small
handwriting and reread it several times imagining a
little dark haired woman composing the mysterious
words. Chills raced down my spine. I wanted to take it
back to Penny Anne but somehow I knew I would not.
The last words were in some foreign language that left
me clueless. How the hell was I supposed to use the

Internet to translate that? I needed someone to help me. Someone I could trust.

In the meantime, I dug around my closet looking for a piece of silk. I remembered our receptionist at work who spoke in grave tones about the etiquette of such things as tarot cards and dreamcatchers. We all thought she was crazy. I wished I had listened more closely. I did recall something about her using silk to protect her cards. It kept things pure and clean. So much for the blue silk blouse that Mac brought me from China. I never wore it anyway. How could I when it was two sizes too small? I pulled it from the hanger, held it up in front of me, and ripped it in two by the neckline in one fierce motion. The fabric stuttered loudly as the threads snapped apart.

Now for the translation. I picked up the phone and dialed Olivia.

CHAPTER THREE

Olivia was bubbling over about having St. Anne. She had decided to incorporate her into the wedding. I imagined her looking so scholarly in her horn rimmed glasses explaining St. Anne to the non-denominational minister that Kevin had insisted on. Olivia knows her stuff. She has that "I have read every book worth reading" look down.

Today, she anxiously jumped about from one wedding detail to another. I found it difficult to follow her train of thought. Somewhere between locations and wines I interrupted to tell her about my latest visit to the antique store. When I described the note and the translation that I needed her help with, she became very quiet.

"Are you okay, Olivia?" I asked. We rarely had strained silences between us. This was unusual.

"I'm just so overwhelmed with planning my wedding," she said and hesitated, "and I miss you. Would you come down and spend the weekend with us? We're having a dinner party tonight. We'll figure out the translation tomorrow. I know someone who can help us."

I agreed to come if she would dress me from her

wonderful wardrobe. Olivia and I looked like sisters and were close to the same size, well we used to be. It was almost spooky, we could have been twins. Sometimes we even dressed alike. She loved leopard print and once we had a three-outfit leopard twin day. Yes, that's right, breakfast, lunch and dinner! She was the sister I never had.

With stop and go traffic on the freeway, I had time to question why I was joining Olivia and Kevin. I didn't think Kevin liked me at all. Twenty years my senior, he was so intimidating. Plus, he was always asking me questions about my job. I hated my job. I finally told him that one night at the dinner table and ultimately broke down in tears. Kevin didn't flinch. He stared at me blankly for a moment, then started a conversation with someone else as if it had never happened. I ended up leaving the dinner table feeling empty. It was uncomfortable for Olivia but she always remained quiet.

Despite my worries, my whole attitude changed as I drove through the gates of Olivia's home. It was an enchanted castle and Olivia was the queen. Her chef, Jason greeted me at the door and showed me to my room where there were roses and chocolates waiting for me. Olivia then made her entrance and after hugging hello, we headed upstairs so she could show me where she'd placed St. Anne. I felt a chill as I approached the landing. Straight ahead of me, on a black lacquered rectangular table was a seven foot carved Buddha from Thailand. It was stunning. In the hands of the Buddha sat my old friend, St. Anne.

Olivia's excitement was in her voice. "Isn't it perfect? It's as if it was made for her!"

I nodded as I walked towards St. Anne and whispered quietly, "I miss you."

"I have not forgotten you."

It was heavenly to hear her voice. Suddenly I became very peaceful, as if all the stress of the past few days had been removed from my body. I bent down and touched the floor with my hands—something I could never do. Closing my eyes, I took a deep breath and slowly exhaled. I opened my eyes to see Olivia beaming at me.

The dinner party was pleasantly uneventful. Excusing myself after dessert I retired to my room. I slept like a baby and woke up the next morning feeling completely renewed. After breakfast, while superman Kevin was playing golf, Olivia called Monique, her language connection. Monique was actually French but spoke several languages. She taught yoga classes and did massage therapy at a local hotel. I had only met her once, but she and Olivia really seemed to click. They chatted briefly, then Olivia hung up the phone and announced that Monique would meet us at noon at the hotel.

Olivia turned her attention to the note. Twirling a lock of long red hair between her graceful manicured fingers, the stunning rock of an engagement ring flashed and her lips pursed. She did not say a word. It reminded me of her strange silence on the previous day. I waited until she was ready to speak.

"This could be Russian. Monique will know. I am very excited for you but the truth is, I'm just feeling really lost right now. I have been working with Florence Shin's book on positive thinking and it is helping a bit. When I was in the business world I felt so powerful but so unfulfilled. Maharaj-ji, a guru from India, speaks of unconditional love. He says God loves us not because we are achievers but because we are on the path. I have been on the path for a lot of years now. It feels like I'm waiting for something to happen. I know, I have Kevin and all the security one could want but I think I am bored a lot of the time. I have done nothing but read self-help books for the last ten years. I just want to know what I'm here for. Do you know how many people spend their lives hoping for what you are being offered here?"

"Olivia, I don't know what to make of all this. All I have ever thought about is keeping a job and avoiding my mother. Now, I'm interested in knowing who I am."

"Welcome to Gandhi's path of the heart." Olivia waved the note in the air. "This note says you are to find seven sacred objects and do some kind of ceremony with seven women. That is amazing. You should read *A Course in Miracles*. You have something special to do. I just wish I did not feel so stuck."

"I was feeling totally lost but since I was given St. Anne I feel better and even giving it to you didn't diminish that. Maybe the answers are not in all those books. Something is happening to me that I don't understand. I was so unhappy that I was willing to just go for it. To me you have always been Cinderella. Your life is beautiful. You have everything plus you are marrying the king of the castle." I stopped for a moment and thought about the man in my life. "I think I'm going to stop seeing Mac."

She loved thinking of herself as Cinderella and agreed with the Mac decision. He was never fully available for a real relationship. Most of the time I felt I was just forcing things.

"Good. Don't beg for love Molly. You have to insist on E.S.P.—available Emotionally, Spiritually and Physically."

That made sense and helped me finalize my decision to end my relationship with Mac. We continued the conversation about Mac until it was time to leave to meet Monique.

Tall, blonde and beautiful—when Monique walked into a room people noticed. And then she had that French accent, a real man magnet. Monique didn't seem to notice the stir she caused in the room, just kissed each of us on both cheeks and gracefully took her seat. Olivia got right down to business (thankfully because I was about to burst at the seams) and told Monique about St. Anne as she pulled her out of her purse.

Seeing my surprised reaction she said, "She wanted to come and meet Monique."

"Of course she did," I said laughing.

I handed the cards and note to Monique as Olivia briefly explained how I'd acquired them. Monique seemed very familiar with the cards as she handled them. She had experimented with the occult in her teens and had played with similar cards.

Opening the note, she scanned it and said, "First of all, this is Russian. The translation is easy: The purple cross forever reigns. The time and place have all been planned. You are a Rose."

"Wow! You have a job to do," Olivia burst out, "she even calls you by name. Yes, I would say that there's an adventure here. Let's pull some cards."

Monique quickly shuffled the cards and pulled: *There is a dark haired woman, mild and susceptible.*

"That's you," Olivia said, smiling at me.

Olivia drew: *A dinner, or an evening party.*

My card was: *News from across the water.* It was like a fortune cookie.

"For someone who grew up with no religion, I would say you are on a holy mission now." Monique had a grin from ear to ear.

"Are you psychic, Monique?"

"Oh I don't like that word. I do have good intuition though." She rose to head back to work and left us with those enchanting double kisses. Olivia and I decided to have a coffee and dessert.

"Every mystery needs new clothes. I have some things for you, so let's go back to the house before Kevin gets home. He gets nervous when I start giving things away."

Poor Kevin. Olivia, as long as I had known her, always gave things away. There was not a more generous person in the world. I wondered if he'd ever get used to it. She paid the check and we headed back to her castle.

I sat in one of her walk-in closets while Olivia pulled out clothes, shoes, handbags and lingerie. I walked out with luggage filled with Prada, Gucci and La Perla.

"Olivia, what do you know about the seven sins? You grew up Catholic. Are there seven saints too?"

"There are seven sins that have been written about through the ages. There are hundreds of saints. Google all this and see what you get. There are many books on the saints too. You should download some but you'd best get out of here now before Kevin sees all of these suitcases!"

She helped me to my car at lightning speed. I drove out just as Kevin drove in. That was close. I almost hit the gate on my way out. My head was spinning. I forgot to say goodbye to St. Anne.

"Bye, Anne!" I yelled out the window.

"I will protect you."

"What about the parking ticket? Where were you then?"

"The past is over."

"When did it end?"

"One half second ago."

I looked in my purse in case she had been placed in my bag. No. I quickly dialed Olivia on her cell but the voicemail picked up.

"Olivia, she's talking to me. Is she in my car somewhere?"

"No."

My mind was racing. This was all really strange. Was I losing my marbles? I parked and started going through the car. The voice wouldn't stop.

"Be at peace. I will protect you."

I closed up the back of my car and began the drive back to Los Angeles, turning on the radio to keep my mind from getting too crazy. It occurred to me that I had to go back to work the following day and I could hardly stand the thought of that. The music of Adele soothed me until I almost ran into the back of a white limousine. I screeched to a stop and caught an angry glare from the driver. The vanity license plate read YNOT7.

My mind started working, digesting the words on the license plate.

Seven saints for seven sins. Okay, there were seven. YNOT7? This was getting really spooky.

My phone rang, startling me. It was Olivia calling to assure me that St. Anne was having her private audience with the Buddha. I told her about the limo and she lapped it up.

"I knew this was going to be fun. I'm getting chills. I think you'd better go over that message very carefully. I wonder who Henry is who told Helena how important this mission is to our future? You have been chosen. I always wanted it to be me, but it's you. I will help you. I will find a way of joining you on this adventure, mark my words. Anne was singing after you left. I heard the most angelic hum, and as I started moving towards the Buddha it stopped. When I turned around it started again. I was going back and forth when Kevin walked in. He thinks the two of us are totally crazy."

Her voice suddenly became very serious. "Don't freak out but I have this feeling that you need to be very careful. If you find anything else, promise me you'll bring it here? We have security. I'm worried about your safety. Not sure why, but you know how I am."

Olivia was not known for her premonitions but occasionally had been correct. I shook it off immediately. For someone so grounded in her intellect she seemed connected at times in ways I could never understand.

"That is so ridiculous. Who would want to harm

me? I have nothing. I own nothing. I have a crappy job and nothing but debt."

"Listen to me please. Read some Doreen Virtue. Something is happening that is not of this world. She says you must listen to the messages and watch for the signs from the angels. I've been reading about all of this for years and I have tried to talk to you about it but you were not open to any of it."

How could I argue with her? The signs were there. Of course I wanted to deny it, but this time I knew I could not. When I was a child, I would often look out at the moon and stars at night and feel the pull of something. Back then, I somehow knew that I was here for something special. My childhood was totally chaotic but I was always taken care of, as if someone was truly watching over me. I wanted to believe that my life was with purpose. I mean, don't we all?

"Okay. Of course. I'll be careful. I promise. Thank you. I love you," I said as I hung up.

I had little shivers going up and down my spine. I glanced over at the cards in their silk wrap in my purse and felt a wave of excitement because my car was filled with secrets. My life was suddenly getting interesting.

When I checked my voicemail I found an unexpected message from The Peninsula Hotel confirming dinner reservations for Tuesday night. Odd. Mac must have made reservations. What an unusual choice. He was up to something. Maybe I had been wrong about him. Maybe he was going to propose. Oh my God! Mac and I had been dating for seven months or was it eight? Well if you didn't count the party we met at, it was seven.

Seven… YNOT7? That must be what this was all about. Oh my God. I didn't think I was ready for this. What was I going to wear? Then I remembered my car full of clothes and laughed. I was going to really surprise him on Tuesday.

As I walked into my apartment building in West

Hollywood I was greeted by Mama, a six-foot-three-inch transvestite dressed to kill. It was "Red Night" at a local gay bar and everyone in my building was going. I passed many blurs of red as I hurried to my apartment on the second floor.

When I walked in, my jaw dropped. My apartment was in shambles. The furniture had been tipped over, all of the cabinet doors were flung open, drawers had literally been yanked from their sockets. Panic rose from the pit of my stomach. Who did this? Were they still here? I slowly backed out of the front door and called the police. Stunned, I sat down on the carpet in the hallway as more blurs of red whizzed past. After about twenty minutes two officers arrived. One entered to check my apartment and the other stayed outside to ask me questions.

"Was your door locked?"

"Yes, I unlocked it to get in."

A few minutes later the first officer walked out and told us it was safe to go in. There did not seem to be any forced entry. I looked around, nothing was missing that I could see. It was a complete wreck, but nothing was missing. I had a sneaky feeling the officers did not believe my story. They finally left and I called the building manager. There were cameras in various parts of the building so it was possible that they caught a glimpse of whoever was in my apartment. He promised to check it out and let me know. It didn't sound like he believed me either.

When you are invaded it seems unreal—like a dream. I wandered around my house picking things up with a strange sense of peace. As if this break in was supposed to have happened. As if I had asked for proof.

CHAPTER FOUR

Work. I never missed a day. I hated it. Every day I was abused. It was the entertainment business in Los Angeles. My boss, an uber famous producer, had zero people skills. I was his right hand and his left and I was bleeding, often working sixty-plus hours a week. But I was doing a job everyone wanted so I pretended to those around me that it was fabulous. The facade got harder and harder to maintain. I wanted out.

Tuesday morning I knew it was one of those weeks that would seem like a month. No word from Mac about the dinner reservations. After work I called him and got no answer, not even his machine, which seemed odd. I assumed it was all just a big surprise. Taking out the clothes from Olivia, I chose a green suede suit. It was a cool evening and the leather felt protective. I put extra care into my hair and makeup. On my way out the door I had this urge to change my clothes. I was going to be late if I took too much longer.

I hurried back to my room. Right on top of the pile of Olivia hand-me-downs was the cobalt blue dress she'd brought back from Australia. It was decorated with the words of a poem written by the Persian poet Rumi. The entire poem repeated itself all over the dress in silkscreened yellow ink. Once I had the dress on I felt complete. I looked sensational. I might even say yes to Mac, I thought as I floated out the front door.

The weather had changed and the skies of sunny California turned gray, opened up and wept. I headed for the parking lot in the pouring rain jumping over puddles in my high heels and landed in my car. Guess suede would have been a bad idea. Thank you, Anne.

"Bless you."

The Peninsula Hotel was not my style. Certainly not very much like Mac either, but it seemed like there were changes in the air and maybe, just maybe, everyone was wrong about him. Especially me. I passed through the narrow bar, which was peppered with the beautiful ones. Women who had their identity tied too closely to beauty and plenty of men on the hunt for the next mistress. I felt all of their eyes on me and started to lose my temporary confidence as I moved through the sea of saline breasts and over-filled lips toward the restaurant. It was gross.

I was running at least ten minutes late so I picked up my pace. I scanned the dining room for Mac. No Mac. Checking in with the hostess, I was met with a look of confusion. There was no reservation.

"Are you sure? I received a phone call."

The hostess dryly informed me that they could not possibly have called, then looked over my shoulder to greet a sable-trimmed woman by name. I was dismissed. The place was crowded. I was hungry and at this point really questioning my sanity.

I must have looked upset because an experienced waiter mercifully pulled me aside and showed me to another room which looked like an elegant living room dressed tastefully in ivory and soft golden hues. He motioned me towards a comfortable couch by the fireplace.

"I think you will be much happier here, Madame." He put a menu on the coffee table in front of me and left.

He was right. Warm and cozy by the fire, I took a moment to absorb my surroundings. I was the only person in the large room. There were relaxed areas of seating throughout. Couches and coffee tables interspersed with dining tables and chairs all set to welcome the weary traveler or the gathering group of friends. I could faintly hear the throng in the bar. There was a pianist playing softly at the back of the room. Huge crystal vases with white roses spilling out were everywhere, and smaller ones had been placed on each table. I don't think I've ever seen so many roses in one place.

I was lost in the scent of rose petals when a waiter breezed by me with the most mouth-watering plate of food. Then the dessert tray rolled by. I was salivating.

Two thoughts came to mind:

1. I was so naive to think that Mac actually made reservations at a place like this.
2. How was I going to pay for this?

I called Mac again. His roommate answered and reminded me that Mac was out of the country on a story. My hunch was correct. I hung up, deflated. What was I not getting here?

The kind waiter brought me a glass of champagne and winked. He asked me if I'd like to order some food. Opening the menu, I took a deep breath. I was here in this dreamy place and I looked amazing. Why not enjoy myself?

"I'll have the filet mignon."

"Excellent choice, Madame, and how would you like it cooked?"

"Medium rare, please."

"Thank you, Madame."

I felt like a rock star. As I waited for my dinner, I thought of Anne. Funny. Every time I even thought about her I felt calmer. She gave me such peace.

When the waiter returned with my dinner, he also delivered a fresh glass of champagne. I hadn't realized I had finished the first one, but he did. He asked me if I would like anything else and just as he was leaving informed me that my dinner check had been taken care of.

A little bewildered, I was also famished, so I dove into the steak while I tried to wrap my head around all of this. Only I couldn't because I was a bit giddy from the champagne. The more I drank, the more comical my whole situation became. By the time I'd finished the steak and the second glass of champagne, I was giggling at the absurdity of it all. Here I was sitting by myself in the middle of the lobby dining like a queen on someone else's dime when I came here thinking I was going to be proposed to!

Caught up in my own comedy, I didn't see the man standing at the end of the couch until he spoke. "It is such a delight to see a young lady enjoying herself. Good evening, my name is Karim Ahmadi. Have you enjoyed your dinner?"

His demeanor was the same as my waiter's. His dark hair was slicked back and he wore a beautiful custom made black suit. I'd say he was just under six feet tall and appeared to be in his early fifties.

"Yes, very nice, Mr. Ahmadi." At this point I wasn't sure if he worked for the hotel or not.

"Good," he said, seeming pleased with himself. "Would you like dessert? Perhaps a coffee or a liqueur?" As he asked this the waiter approached, right on cue.

Considering for just a moment, I looked at my empty second glass of champagne, "Yes, I'd love a cup of coffee please."

The waiter then turned his attention to Mr. Ahmadi. "And for you, Sir?"

He ordered a dessert for both of us and some fancy

after dinner drink that I couldn't understand the name of. The waiter nodded and disappeared. Mr. Ahmadi calmly sat down on the sofa across from me. I wasn't sure what to make of this presumptuous man. All of a sudden I felt uncomfortable and changed my mind about the coffee. I mumbled something about the check and started to stand up to call the waiter back when he stopped me.

"Miss, please. I'm sorry if I startled you. Do you mind me joining you? I saw how upset you were. A lover deserted... been there myself. This is all my treat. It's my pleasure, besides it is a business expense for me," he said as his eyes twinkled and he smiled warmly. "Now please, sit down and tell me a bit about yourself. What is your name?"

I hesitantly sat back down, "Molly."

"Pleasure to meet you, Miss Molly. And what does the forlorn but still lovely Miss Molly who walks around with a poem on her dress do?"

He had such a gentle demeanor and compassionate eyes. I decided he was safe.

"I am an assistant to a producer."

"Of course. And you are waiting for your acting career to explode. Right?"

I chuckled at the thought of that. "No. I've never wanted to be an actor. I just like helping people. But I think I'm getting over that with this job."

The waiter dropped off our order, bowed slightly and quietly left. We continued to chat as we nibbled on the divine desserts.

"So. Are you looking for a job?" he queried.

"No. Well—yes, but not really looking. I haven't had time to look."

"Great. I have a job for you."

I sobered up instantly.

"Wait a minute. You realized my plight and bought me dinner. Thank you. But seriously, how can you offer me a job? You don't even know me." I shifted on my seat while examining the Paisley print on his tie.

"You are correct about that to a point. You see… I read people. I know people. That is my skill. You are good people. You are an angel. In the Koran angels are very important."

"You can't be serious?"

"Miss Molly, I'm an attorney and I can assure you I am quite serious. I have a client who is British. The company is looking for a courier to deliver legal documents. I am actually in town interviewing potential candidates. The pay is very generous. The president is a kind woman and is looking for someone she can trust. She will pay five thousand dollars up front and a set fee for each delivery, depending on where it needs to go and the time involved. You must follow the instructions given to the letter and not ask any more questions than necessary."

Oh my God, he was serious.

"Is this honest? I wouldn't even consider doing something illegal."

"I am as I said—an attorney. Here is my card. You can think about it and call me if you want the job. Madame's present courier has been with her for twenty-five years and is retiring. She is very particular. You cannot miss flights or appointments. You were ten minutes late for your dinner."

"You noticed that? Well I am rarely late. In fact, I have a reputation for being early. Many friends say it is because I'm a Virgo? Do you know what that means?"

He grinned. "Yes I do. September fifth!"

"I'm the twenty-sixth of August. Okay. So you know. It's a deal. Yes. Tell me more about this job…. it involves travel? That's wonderful. I'm so ready for a change. I seem to work well with Virgos."

I was probably the only non-neat freak Virgo I knew. What was it with this astrology anyway? I thought as he responded to each of my questions. At some point I realized it was getting late and decided it was time to make my exit.

"Thank you again for everything, Mr. Ahmadi. I'm afraid I really must head home now. I appreciate you for considering me for this job. I'll think about it and let you know," I said, standing up.

He stood to join me. "Call me at the end of the week and tell me when you're ready to start. I'll give you all the details then, Miss Molly."

Was he reading my mind? How did he know I was going to take the job?

"Rose. Molly Rose." I stretched out my hand.

"Good evening, Miss Rose. Drive home carefully. Keep your angel wings in the car."

I was barely able to concentrate on the road as I drove home. Erupting with excitement, I stopped at the first traffic light and yelled out the window, "I'm going to quit my job! I'm moving on! Thank you, Anne!" I swear I could feel God at work.

"It is time."

CHAPTER FIVE

I woke up the following day unsure if the night before was merely a dream. There, sitting on my bedside table was Mr. Ahmadi's card. It was right next to the silk-wrapped deck of cards Penny Anne had given me. Not a dream. Carefully unwrapping the cards, I decided to take a card from the center of the deck just for kicks. The card read: *It is time for a new beginning.*

Jeez, how many messages did I need? It was time to quit my job.

I drove over to my boss's Beverly Wilshire penthouse suite, sat down on one of his three brown leather couches and gave him my two weeks' notice. He yelled at me, demanding that I pack my desk and leave. He also mentioned that he saw me with my new rich boyfriend at The Peninsula Hotel. That explained the phone call. I completely forgot that I had made a reservation for him months before. But it still didn't explain my encounter with Mr. Ahmadi.

"Ah by the way, Molly, do you have any cigarettes you can leave? Got a couple of actors coming in who smoke and you always take care of that."

"Sure."

As soon as I got back to my desk, a woman from

Human Resources came in to give me my exit pass and collect anything confidential I might have. All I had left to do was pack up seven years of photos, memories and a half-dozen different packages of cigarettes. I didn't smoke, but I always carried them in my purse to "loan" them to co-workers and talent. Cigs were the best way to make friends and keep them. I left a few packs on my desk as I walked out so the next person might have a chance with this group.

Leaving the building I instantly felt better. As soon as I started my car I called Mr. Ahmadi. The pleasant voice of the receptionist took my call back information. The rest of the day went by without a return call.

The next day—no return call.

Four more days went by.

I started madly cleaning my apartment. Using toothpaste to clean the shower grout, I thought about calling my now ex-boss and begging him to rehire me. I had absolutely no idea who Mr. Ahmadi really was. What was I thinking? I felt silly that I'd believed him. On the other hand, I was completely relieved to be away from that job. A huge weight had been lifted from my shoulders. I was out from under a rock for the first time in years. No, I wouldn't go back. My grandma always told me, "A good horse never eats the grass behind it."

I stopped to check my bank balance. Not good. Rent was due in two weeks. I would need additional funds.

I was down on my knees cleaning floorboards in my living room when an idea came to me. One of my neighbors was an attorney for the state. I could ask him to check out Mr. Ahmadi. I called his cell phone and started to leave a message but got cut off. After getting put on hold three times by his office, I became so frustrated that I threw my cell phone across the room. Thankfully, it landed on my bed near a pillow. I pulled out the cards from their silk protection, hoping for a message and read: *An enemy; cultivate friends; they will aid you.*

Maybe this was not such a great idea these cards. I pulled out a half gallon tub of vanilla bean ice cream and grabbed a spoon.

The phone rang and I pounced on it, knowing it had to be Mr. Ahmadi.

"What are you doing at home? I was just going to leave you a message."

"Olivia! I quit my job. I met a man at The Peninsula Hotel and he offered me a job."

"Molly, that hotel is a favorite of high class call-girls."

"I know. Don't worry about that. I made a reservation for my boss and forgot and somehow thought it was for me. I met this man, Karim Ahmadi. I've got a neighbor who's an attorney. I'm hoping he can help me find out more about him, but I haven't had a chance to ask him. So much is happening. I'm a little scared actually. I've left messages for Mr. Ahmadi and have not heard back from him. I quit my job. It's so hard to find a job right now. Tons of people I know are looking for jobs. What have I done?"

"Take a deep breath. Let me see what I can find out. I'll put Kevin on it. What's his name again and where does he live? Was he cute?"

"Yes, but no, it's nothing like that. His full name on his business card is Karim L. Ahmadi and he's an attorney in Houston, Texas. Call me as soon as you find out anything. Oh, and my apartment was broken into but nothing taken. The building manager looked at the video footage from the front door but said it was too grainy to really identify anyone."

Olivia launched into a lecture. "I have told you before, I'm not comfortable with your living situation."

"Please stop. I called the alarm company and set up a security system for my place. I'm protected. You know those cards are scaring me a bit. I think the three cards we pulled with Monique pretty much describe my life. Now they tell me I have an enemy."

"Please promise me that you will keep your cell phone by your bed and lock all your doors and turn that alarm on? Do you know the neighbor who lives next to you?"

"I promise. And my next door neighbor is a very nice man who is becoming a woman." I laughed. It felt good to laugh.

"Of course! Remember though, he's still a man till he removes his you know what! Don't worry. I'll find out what I can. Love you," she said as she hung up the phone, laughing.

Just then my doorbell rang. My neighbor bringing me a check for 250 dollars. I had forgotten that I'd picked up groceries and prescriptions for him last month while he was getting his hormone injections. He was wearing one of Oliva's St. John dresses. It looked better on him than it ever did on me.

Less than an hour later Olivia called to tell me that Mr. Ahmadi was an international attorney with a very distinguished clientele. He even represented some of the royals in Europe. Kevin had called a few of his Augusta golfing friends.

"I am with you at all times."

I whispered a prayer of protection as I closed my eyes for the night, something I'd never done. St. Anne must have been rubbing off on me. Who would have thought that giving away something would bring it closer? The phone ringing woke me up.

"Miss Rose? I have Mr. Ahmadi on the line for you."

I could hear my heart thumping as I waited clutching the phone.

"Miss Rose? Karim Ahmadi."

"Yes, Mr. Ahmadi," I said as I tried to steady my voice.

"You may call me Karim."

"Thank you. Please call me Molly."

"Molly, when can you start your new line of work?"

"When would you like me to start? I'm ready to go. I quit my job."

"Wonderful news. Please give all your personal information to my secretary and she'll set you up for the first delivery. Expect your ticket with all instructions to come via FedEx. The advance money I mentioned during our conversation at the hotel will be wired to your account in one week."

A week went by before the FedEx came. A ticket to Paris! I had two days to prepare myself. The ticket was enclosed along with an itinerary reflecting hotel reservations and car service. Three nights at the Hotel Raphael. I checked my bank account and the advance was there. I was swooning.

I'd only been to Paris once when I was five years old. That was the year my parents divorced. A year later, my father died. My mother married the first man she met and then the next man and the next until she met and finally married Dr. Bob Johnson, an officer in the Air Force stationed in Budapest, Hungary. My mother and I were never close. I learned to survive. She had a sister, Sally, who lived in Idaho. I spent time with her on weekends as a child, but since I'd moved to Los Angeles I rarely saw her.

Another phone call snapped me out of my reflection. My ex-boss's new assistant proudly telling me my check was ready for pickup.

"Divine timing."

CHAPTER SIX

Getting ready to go to Europe in two days would have been impossible, had Olivia not given me the suitcase and the clothes. I was set. I finished packing by two p.m. so I cruised over to Melrose on my bike. I had to find out—was the gypsy who gave the St. Anne relic and cards to Penny Anne still alive?

I entered the shop where Penny Anne once again was tending her private bar. Exactly why I rode my bike instead of driving.

"Well, Molly Rose, my long lost friend! What can I make for you, darlin'? I have a wonderful drink I'm about to mix up right this minute, a Scarlett O'Hara. It's one my mama used to make for my step daddy. Sweetie, perhaps I should make you a Green Goddamn for dressing like that."

"Just jeans today," I said.

"Well if you're wearing jeans at least show some style and put on some high heels. They give an alluring line to the leg and put that undeniable come-hither sway in your walk. Of course, we Southern women exaggerate that wiggle—especially when the occasion calls for it! You should wear brighter colors too. You have such pretty eyes."

Her comments reminded me of my mother giving her regular advice. Penny Anne had nothing to gain from these suggestions, she just seemed to be trying to help. It was entirely possible that my mother was just trying to be helpful too. I honestly didn't know whether I should say thank you or I'm sorry. I just smiled and waited for my drink.

"I beg your pardon?" She arched a warning eyebrow and threw an indignant hand on her slim hip.

It took me a second to get her gist, "Oh, a Scarlet O'Hara please, ma'am."

"Now, that's more like it, Missy."

"I'm off to Paris tomorrow."

"Oh mercy, you are blessed. What time?"

"Three-thirty."

"Well you've got plenty of time then, honey. Here you go now. Enjoy!" She handed me a bright pink glass with a small green umbrella and clear straw.

"Do you think that the woman who sold you the relic is still in Paris?"

"I cannot imagine her being anywhere else. I highly doubt that little hen has the wherewithal to move."

"You think I could find her?"

"Of course, darlin'. I'll never forget that one. She lived on the Rue de Bac, real close to a little chapel. Her apartment was on the ground floor. As I recall, she had a lot of colored glass in the window. I'm not sure if she's still in the same apartment but just go and see if you can find her. Are you sure you are not Southern?"

"I'm fairly certain of that, Penny Anne. I grew up in Idaho. My mom was raised in Idaho and my dad lived overseas during his childhood. Why do you ask?"

"Well dear, Southern women are not bystanders in life. We're avid participants who grab our destiny by the neck and choke the life we want out of it. Go for it, girlfriend, but please do wear heels."

I loved Penny Anne's attitude.

"What's her name?"

"Oh, Lordy, I don't know. I do have to tell you that she's a bit sour. That, I so vividly recall. Full of vinegar. She was certainly a sight to behold. I could never figure out how old she was either. She's an odd one. You know more flies are caught with honey than with vinegar, right?"

I nodded and pressed on with the task at hand.

"I need to find out more about the relics. I just have to know more. Are you Catholic?"

"Oh, good Lord no. My father was a Methodist and his father before him. As far as we know, and believe me Southern women keep track of their heritage, we've always been Methodists."

"I need to understand why the St. Anne had to come home with me. Why me?"

"Now that is worth investigating, darlin'. Go to the churches when you're in Paris. The great ones are there and I believe they were built because of relics. Yes, I believe that is what I heard. Ask around and someone will tell you. But look pretty. Always use make up to look your best before you go out hunting for information. Bon voyage, sweetie!" She raised her glass high.

I was glad I only had one of those drinks. It was too sweet and packed a punch. I walked my bike home.

The next day, I checked in at the airport and was just settling in to *People* magazine when I heard my name called over the loudspeaker. The woman on the other end of the red courtesy phone instructed me to come to the Air France lounge. Upon entering and giving my name, a petite nondescript blonde in her early sixties approached me with a large yellow envelope.

"Hello, Miss Rose. I'm Emily Eaves. We work for the same company. I've done your job for a time and I am ready to retire. I'm passing along the baton to you now." Her accent was distinctly British and there was a hint of sadness in her eyes.

Extending the envelope to me she continued, "Inside this envelope is the package you'll deliver. Also enclosed you'll find credit cards for your expenses, cash and some traveler's checks. There is a cell phone with instructions attached. The package must be delivered tomorrow at three p.m. Mr. Philippe Dubois will meet you at the Hemingway Bar in the Ritz Hotel. I highly recommend you sit at the bar and have something to drink. Prepare to wait. He's usually late, but please do not be late yourself. Do you have any questions?"

"It's so mysterious, Emily. Is it legal?"

"Oh yes. Just large transactions that require privacy. Perfectly legal. It has been a privilege for me, really. Oh, you'll travel Business Class. May I see your tickets please?"

Looking over my tickets, she seemed content.

"Yes, everything is in order. And, Miss Rose, one more thing. If you'd like to extend your stay you may do that, at your own expense of course."

"Good to know. How often do you think I'll be traveling?"

"With the way things have been—I would count on one trip per month. Madame is highly enterprising."

I boarded the plane with the large yellow envelope tucked tightly under my arm. I didn't want it out of my sight. I had seat 61A. I must remember to get an aisle seat next time. I hated to feel closed in. Sitting next to me was a very good-looking older man, but he barely looked my way until the flight attendant took our beverage orders. I asked for a white wine and he looked at me briefly, raising his perfectly trimmed eyebrows and gazing at me above his reading glasses.

"Hi, I'm Molly," I said, offering my hand.

"Jim," he grunted at me and went back to reading his *Wall Street Journal* without shaking my hand.

The flight was surprisingly fast. My Air France Airbus landed with a thump, a chirp of rubber and the roar of reverse thrusting engines. It wasn't until then that Jim asked me why I was in Paris.

"Vacation," I told him as we taxied to the gate. I avoided the rest of his questions as best I could. As soon as the door opened I was off and running. The travel bag Olivia gave me was perfect. Everything I needed for three days was tucked neatly inside, along with the deck of cards, which I included at the last minute. After Customs, a car was waiting to whisk me off to the City of Lights.

After checking in at the hotel I unpacked, showered and tried to rest. I was overly excited so resting was not an option. The deck of cards wrapped in its silk cocoon was sitting on the bedside table beckoning me. What a perfect way to start off this adventure. I unwrapped the deck and drew a card: *You will be given a gown fit for a queen*.

I had two hours before my meeting at the Ritz. I dressed and hailed a cab. Traffic sounds, bike horns and "bonjours" were all pouring out at me. The driver dropped me off at the Ritz. Hungry, I strolled around the area following my nose. Stopping at a crepe stand I ordered a plain cheese crepe and watched them make it. Quickly eating the "crepe fromage" as they called it, I meandered over to the Place Vendome to look around and check out the couture houses. I had promised to take some pictures of the current Paris trends for Olivia.

First stop—Louis Vuitton. A beautiful sales girl welcomed me in English. Damn! She knew. I'd hoped to look a little French in my black and white outfit. When she found out where I was from she lit up and introduced herself. Chantal loved California and thought of Los Angeles as Hollywood, packed wall-to-wall with movie stars. Her cousin from San Francisco was visiting, so she invited me to join them for dinner the following evening. I agreed. We exchanged numbers and she said she would text me the address. Kiss kiss.

I crossed into the luxury of the lobby of the Ritz, following directions to the famous bar. George Clooney was sitting there with three other guys. He smiled at me as I passed. Now I knew I was in the perfect place. I still had twenty minutes so I ordered some mineral water. Way too early for me to have any alcohol. Besides, I had to find that gypsy.

Then, the weirdest thing happened. Jim, the unfriendly guy from the plane, walked in and parked himself right next to me. He took the only empty seat, which made me a bit uneasy. I wanted to be sure that Mr. Dubois could find me. Jim said hello and began asking me questions about my trip. I froze up. Something was off. I couldn't put my finger on it, but I didn't feel comfortable sharing anything with this guy. He asked me where I was staying.

"By the airport... I can't remember the name of the hotel," I told him nonchalantly.

I wanted him to leave and give me the extra seat back. After about forty-five agonizing minutes of interrogation (I couldn't tell if he was trying to pick me up or was just nosey) he nodded to someone who took his seat. Mr. Dubois. They knew each other!

"Miss Rose, please don't be offended but we must make sure you are trustworthy. Mr. Jim Thoreau works for us too. Rest assured that we intend to keep our business strictly confidential," explained Mr. Dubois in perfect English despite his heavy French accent.

I guess I passed the test. I was getting almost rude with Mr. Jim Thoreau. I handed Mr. Dubois the yellow envelope and he gave me a small blue bag with ribboned handles.

"It is a gift from Madame. Good afternoon, Miss Rose." He nodded and left.

I lifted out the contents of the bag, a blue box with a gold fleur de lis holding a bottle of liquor. Chambord black raspberry liquor. It felt special.

George Clooney smiled at me again as I was leaving.

"Have a great time," I offered up flirtatiously.

"Hey, you're American?"

"Yes, from Los Angeles."

Winking, he told me he was from Los Angeles too. Funny guy. Where else would he be from?

"Would you like to join us for a drink?"

"No, thank you," I heard myself saying as I sauntered out. I thought of Penny Anne as I put a little extra sway in my walk.

Holy shit, I just turned George Clooney down! Olivia would never believe that I turned George down. No one would believe this one. I had a better chance of having them believe the relic was speaking to me. I giggled with delight as I headed out to find the gypsy.

CHAPTER SEVEN

The sun was beginning to set as I hurried over to the Rue de Bac. There was a small sign with an arrow pointing to the Chapel of the Miraculous Medal. A woman crossed the street with six children of various ages. They entered an iron gate into a compound and yes, the window had lots of colored glass.

"Hello!" I yelled out as she was opening the gate.

She turned and looked at me with alarm on her face, shooing the children in through the gate. I ran across the street in front of traffic to stop her but she slammed the iron gate in my face.

"I no take nothing! I no steal from you! These good children!" she barked at me through the gate.

"Wait. Please. I don't think someone as lovely as you would steal anything. I just want to ask you some questions about a relic."

"What relic? Where you from?"

"St. Anne. You sold it to a woman from the United States."

"I no understand, relic."

I stood looking through the iron bars at the ageless woman. She was dressed in brightly colored clothes and her amber eyes were fiery as she shouted at me. I began to whisper to soothe her.

"Please... you sold it to a Southern woman, Penny Anne Saylor. She sent me to you."

"You show me this so-called relic."

"I don't have it with me. It's back home."

"How I supposed to believe? I no have time. I busy woman. Go. You leave." She turned and started to walk away.

"Please. Please. Where did it come from? Please!"

Pausing for a moment, she reconsidered and turned around.

"You wait there," she pointed to the sidewalk in front of her gate.

I waited for about twenty minutes and wasn't giving up. I'm not Southern, but I was going to act as if I was. Penny Anne told me to use honey.

"You come now quick inside!"

She opened the gate, hastily locking it behind me, and ushered me into a tiny dark space filled with her collections. Garbage bags full. Things stacked on top of things. Pillows, bowling balls, china, shoes, vases, Christmas ornaments, well you name it she had it and more. I held my hand over my nose to protect myself from the smell.

"You have some beautiful things," I lied sweetly.

"What you need? What you want to buy? For you I give good price." She went straight for the sale, delighted to have me as her prisoner. Her eyes were dancing now.

"Do you have any more relics?"

"Relics not sold, must give. Only sell thecas."

"What is a theca?"

"The case. Relic always gift. Nice gift, yes?"

"Yes, very nice gift. Do you have any thecas?"

"Maybe one here. I know special one but not here. You go South?"

"What do you mean?"

"South France. Many nice places South. What else

you buy?"

"Where did the relic of St. Anne come from?"

"Her body. Bone from arm."

"Yes, but where did you find it?"

"My cousin in Yugoslavia. Long time ago. She said bring bad luck, must sell right away. Seem like long time pass since that day! Now I have much to sell. Thanks be to God. I find something for you now. You wait here! No touch my things!" She disappeared in a puff of dust.

"Of course not. I'll just wait here for you."

My eyes wandered again over the glass vases, linens, a collection of Cuckoo clocks all with different times. A real warehouse of junk. Cobwebs on every corner, filth everywhere.

The gypsy suddenly reappeared carrying a long robe. Thousands of golden beads and delicate embroidery of angels covered both the back and sides. Fashioned from red silk velvet it was sewn together with what looked like real gold thread.

"This for you, yes? You go to church?"

"Me? No. It looks like it's for a priest." I was astonished at what she'd dug out from her yard of bones.

"Oh, no priest wear this robe. This vestment of Pope. Very old. Many say he was woman. No woman can be Pope. You put on."

Before I could refuse her she had positioned the robe over my shoulders. It was so heavy it made my shoulders sag. Feeling the weight of responsibility it must have taken to wear this holy piece, I was suddenly transported. I found myself kneeling in a church holding a golden chalice. In front of me, through a huge stained glass window sunbeams were pouring muted colored light on my red velvet slippers. Painted angels were in flight on the ceiling above me.

Then, as quickly as it started, the spell was over. Back amidst the gypsy's hoarding, I could smell cigarette smoke on the fabric of the robe. I felt dizzy. I wanted it off. She helped me remove it. There was no empty chair so I sat on the floor and put my head between my legs to regain myself.

"It must be jet lag," I whispered quietly, looking into her catlike eyes.

"How much?" I asked, surprising myself. What the hell was I doing?

She smiled down at me. "For you, special price. Seven hundred dollars cash. You come back and I look for more." Then she waited.

I opened my silver Prada wallet and counted out the money my mother had just sent me as an Easter gift. I had exactly that much and some euros with me. She brought out a clear plastic garment bag to carry the heavy vestment home in. It covered only the top and the rest was spilling out all over. I hugged it to me with both arms to keep it off the ground. Before I left I asked her for her phone number.

"No! I no give number! Private. You find me when you need special things. I find many special things. Thanks be to God. You need clock?"

I told her that I was not interested in clocks right at this time and wrote my cell phone number on a pink recipe card I found on the floor. I begged her to call me if she found the other relic.

It was too late to see the Chapel of Miracles and I was now burdened with the weight of my new robe. Plus, I had my purse and the blue bag, which I had almost left on the floor. I grabbed a taxi using my leftover euros.

Back at the hotel I carefully arranged the vestment on the bed, stopping for a moment to take in the grandeur of it, afraid to put it on again. It was so well preserved that I wondered if the gypsy was telling the truth about its age. I hung it up in the closet and closed the door. Exhausted, I got ready for bed. On the bedside table the card I'd pulled earlier caught my attention. It might not be a gown, but the robe was definitely fit for a queen.

The next morning I woke up excited. My plan was to visit churches, as Penny Anne had suggested. My new vestment was laid out on the bed on top of me like a comforter. I shook the fog out of my head and hung it back in the closet.

I stopped by the concierge desk and asked about the churches. I had only one day and I knew I wanted to see Notre Dame. The hotty from the front desk was listening in and suggested Sacre-Coeur on the West Side and oddly enough the small Chapelle of our Lady of Miracles, which he called "the motherhouse" and winked at me. He suggested I look for 140 Rue de Bac or I may not find it. He also handed me a flyer for a baroque concert at Saint–Roch Church at ten p.m. tonight. When he handed me the flyer he touched my hand a bit longer than necessary. I exited the hotel with a big smile on my face.

The subway seemed to be the best way to get to the motherhouse. When I got to the top of the subway stairs and looked at a map, I realized I was exactly where I had been the day before. No sign of her highness the gypsy. I walked to 140 Rue de Bac. There was an eight-foot wooden fence surrounding the enclave with no sign. A sister was walking through the gate so I followed her inside.

It was the most beautiful little chapel I'd ever seen. I gasped at a breathtaking white marble statue of Mary, sculpted in 1850. Standing over the altar, she was crowned with twelve stars and rays of light beamed from her outstretched palms to the floor. Exquisite murals and mosaics depicting miracles decorated the walls. Worshippers were standing as well as sitting in the traditional pews. People filled the little church, invisible from the street, and it was only 9:20 a.m. I scanned the room for relics. A sister standing by me nodded, but she didn't understand English.

I found myself standing in line watching those ahead of me fall down in front of the Mary statue. I felt energy moving into my body and as I approached, I was literally pushed down to the floor! Believe me when I say I have never been religious. This caught me off guard. Tears began streaming down my face and I couldn't seem to pull myself together.

A woman next to me, crying too, hugged me. She handed me a medal, the miraculous medal. A young girl named Catherine had apparitions or visitations of the Virgin and a medal was coined and distributed to Parisians during the 1832 Cholera epidemic. Cures and protections were soon reported. Many miracles have come from the use of this medal. I held it up to the light from the windows and marveled at its luminosity. Peace and joy filled me.

Bussing across the city so I could see more of Paris, I reached Notre Dame and made my way into the main chapel. Near the altar was the most beautiful window. Shades of deep blues and reds formed a circular rose-like image. I recognized it as the window I saw when I put on the robe at the gypsy's house. Maybe I'd seen too many postcards. There was a relic tour for ten euros and I gladly paid it. Although all the relics were behind glass, I could still feel their energy. I stopped cold in front of a chalice. Suddenly feeling dizzy, I leaned on a nearby column to steady myself. My chalice! I moved closer to it to read the small signage: *Pope John VIII used this chalice inlaid with amethysts and rubies.*

I walked back to the chapel, slipped into an empty pew and dropped to my knees. "Please God, help me to understand," I whispered.

As a wave of peace moved over my body, I heard the words *Joan, Joan, Joan.* Time passed and I came out of my trance to realize I was still kneeling and staring at the window. I had been here before. I knew it. I felt it. The déjà vu was a reality. That was my chalice! I tried to get back into the relic display with my torn ticket and was told no. You know how the French can be.

Over the hills I walked to the next church, passing some wonderful graffiti. It felt like I was opening up to a whole new level of clarity, as if I'd been asleep for a while. I stopped and listened to the birds singing. I could almost sense what they were saying. The air was crisp and the view was spectacular. I could see my destination, the Sacred Heart, its large white dome glimmering in the sun. Crowds were searching for the Mother.

I was puffing when I reached the basilica as it was atop the highest hill in the Montmarte section of Paris. At the entrance of the church I joined a tour group. The tour guide was talking about relics. My ears perked up as I strained to hear what he was saying.

"The Sacred Heart was built so that people could venerate or pray with the relics of the Virgin."

Was she a real woman, the Virgin Mary? I had not really thought about it before. It seemed to me that she was merely symbolic. Could any person be that good? That loving?

The tour guide was moving his group forward, so I interrupted, asking if I could pay to join them.

He smiled. "A lovely woman may join only if she pays double."

Thinking he was kidding I laughed, but he was serious. I paid him twenty-five euros and we were off. Twelve of us followed our master around the church. He was totally full of himself, sharing way too much information for my liking, but the relics were driving me. As soon as he stopped talking for a few minutes, I asked him what he knew about relics.

"The relic safe at the church is closed now because of terrorists. No entry. Closed."

When I asked him another question about relics he gave me a dirty look and didn't answer. Then when I approached him again he walked away. I left the tour and decided to go to the gift shop where I asked a young sister behind the counter what she knew about relics. She looked at me, shook her head and ignored my questions. Frustrated, I left the church with more questions than I came with.

During dinner with my new friends, all I could think about was the churches. Everyone agreed to go to the concert, so off we went to the Church of Saint-Roch on the Rue Saint-Honore. It was divine and inspiring and just what I needed.

As we said our good-byes, Chantal's cousin whispered in my ear, "You are so special, so spiritual."

"Really? I never think of myself that way," I confessed.

"You are special, Joan. You're so familiar to me. Please stay in touch with me back in Los Angeles." She handed me her card.

"What did you call me? Joan?"

"Oh sorry, my mistake. Molly, right?"

"It is all happening right now."

CHAPTER EIGHT

I caught my flight back to Los Angeles first thing the next morning. Home in my cozy apartment I put on some sweats and unpacked my bags. Carefully pulling out my new vestment, I wondered if I'd been too extravagant. Then I remembered it was a gift. My mom gave me the money to spend on myself.

"What is yours will always come back to you."

Slipping the vestment over my clothes, I went once again into a trance. I was holding the golden chalice, looking at a beautiful stained glass window. I extended my index and middle fingers on my right hand as a blessing. I could smell incense and hear Latin hymns being sung. Light was softly spilling in through the window.

I dropped the robe to the floor in shock. It was a church like Notre Dame. When I picked it up I could feel something in the hem. Finding a slit in the hem, I pushed out a small old key engraved with the fleur de lis. What secret would it unlock?

My life these days seemed full of secrets. Secrets that were beginning to feel quite normal. Who was I working for anyway? It was a great job so I didn't question it, just crashed on my bed and fell fast asleep until a loud knock woke me up. FedEx.

When I signed for the package I noticed a couple standing in the hallway making notes as they looked at my apartment. One of them took a photo of me. I slammed the door shut and opened my package. Damn tourists!

Another trip to Paris in seven days. Same meeting place, same time, but different hotel accommodations. This time I would be staying on the Rue de Bac.

The gypsy must have found the relic. As I looked through the package I knew I would need to stay longer in France so I called and left a message with Blake, Madame's assistant. Within five minutes the acknowledgement came. I made arrangements to extend my ticket and hotel for an extra week.

Olivia called to see how my trip went and I filled her in on all the details. She insisted that I bring the robe to Laguna Beach so it would be safe while I traveled. I couldn't agree more. I needed to get a haircut first and then I would drive down and drop it off.

Now, my stylist always had movie magazines, tons of gossip magazines, and of course *People*, but today on her counter was *U.S. News and World Report*. Pretty unusual. Someone must have left it because Kristin did not keep up with current events. The headline on the right side grabbed my eye: "THE LADY WAS A POPE".

I trembled. The issue was dated July 24, 2000. It was fourteen years old! When Kristin came over to start my haircut I asked her if the magazine was hers.

"Oh no. Someone left that."

"Can I have it?"

"Yeah sure. Take it before I'm forced to burn it to protect my reputation."

I scanned the article as she went to work on my hair. The story is as enduring as it is dubious: A millennium or so ago in Rome, the Pope was riding in a procession when suddenly she—that's right, she—went into labor and had a baby. Nonsense? Europeans in the Middle Ages didn't think so. "The story of a Pope named Joan," writes historian J.N.D. Kelly in his *Oxford Dictionary of Popes*, "was accepted without question in Catholic circles for centuries."

The tale faded in the seventeenth century, but never died. While most Americans apparently have never heard of the story, it has continued to fascinate people across the world. Donna Woolfolk Cross in her historical novel *Pope Joan* suggests that a four hundred year clerical cover-up kept her hero from being recognized as one of history's most famous women.

In his 1999 book *The Legend of Pope Joan*, British writer Peter Stanford reports visiting the Vatican and inspecting an unusual chair inspired by the trouble with Joan. The wooden throne, with a potty-style hole in the seat, is said to have been used until the sixteenth century in the ceremony of papal consecration. According to medieval accounts, each prospective pope would sit on the hole while an examining cleric felt under the seat. A moment later, the examiner would withdraw his hand and solemnly declare, "Our nominee is a man." Stanford, a former editor of London's *Catholic Herald*, argues that Pope Joan was an historical figure, although he doubts some of the story's details. Donna Cross agrees. "Where there's that much historical smoke, there must have been a fire," she says. "Something happened."

Something happened all right. I have her vestment and I saw her chalice!

I carried the magazine out with my new haircut and decided to drive over to Melrose. I was becoming very fond of Penny Anne and I could just imagine how much she'd love my hair. I parked, reapplied my lipstick and put on some mascara. Slipping on some new red heels I grabbed the vestment from my trunk.

Sure enough, cocktails were being served.

"Welcome home, darlin'. I was just about to make a gin fizz. How about it, girlfriend?"

"Not today, I have some driving to do. Thank you. Can I have a rain check?"

"Of course you can, sweetheart. Heavens, don't you look beautiful today all done up? This is what I mean. Honey you come right over here and take this drink off my hands. That's right. Now I'll just make another one and we'll sit and have some civilized conversation. I want to hear all about your trip to Paris. Mercy me, what do you have in that garment bag? Take it out this minute and show me what you've got!"

She gasped and clutched at her collar as I carefully removed the robe.

"That is the real thing, Molly. Where in God's world did you find that—a museum thief?"

"I hope not. I bought it from your gypsy. She insisted it was for me. Isn't it amazing?"

"Beyond amazing, honey. It's supernatural! My guess is that it is twelfth century."

I laughed and realized how much I needed this woman.

I told her about the rest of my trip. I promised to bring the Chambord next time so we could try it with champagne, which of course she had in the icebox at all times. She suggested that I ask the gypsy more about Southern France and take a trip there by train. I agreed and told her I'd already changed my ticket.

"That's my girl," she said with a wink.

I just happened to look at my watch and realized that I was supposed to be on my way to Laguna Beach. Grabbing my vestment, I hugged Penny Anne and sprinted out the door.

Traffic was awful so I ended up arriving thirty minutes past the dinner hour. I called to warn them, but I was sure Kevin would still glare me down when I got there. To my complete surprise, he actually seemed to be in a really good mood. He even complimented my clothes. Of course I was wearing an Olivia original.

After dinner I brought the vestment in from my car. Heading upstairs to Olivia's office I passed St. Anne.

"Bless you."

I stopped and told her all about my experiences. I stood there talking to her for at least twenty minutes or more. Olivia must have heard so she kept Kevin busy downstairs.

"Molly, I'll be right up," she finally called up the stairway. "Can't wait to show you my new office furniture."

She joined me on the upper landing and we headed to her office.

"Would you please put her somewhere more private so we can talk to her without someone seeing us?"

"I tried, but she wants to be right there."

"I think my next saint better not be so picky."

Once we were safely behind closed doors, I unbagged the vestment. Olivia was in shock.

"Molly this is priceless! This belongs in a museum. Can I put it on?"

She did and nothing seemed to happen.

"Wow this is heavy," she sighed.

"I know, I know. Can you keep it for me?"

Olivia lit up. "It has to be here because it's part of the ceremony. It's so amazing that all this is happening. And now you are going to Paris again!"

"I'm going to stay longer this time so I can explore. Any recommendations?"

"Well, France is full of history. I just finished a book about Joan of Arc by Mark Twain."

"Really? Twain wrote a book on Joan of Arc? I had no idea. Do you think she is one of the seven saints?"

"Yes, I do. And I think Twain did too, because apparently he considered it his greatest work. I'm dying to go look at her statues and find out more about her. She reminds me of you."

That night as I slept I had a vivid dream. I was on a horse and there was a raging fire closing in behind us. The horse was galloping as fast as it could while I held on for dear life. Flames were everywhere. I could feel the smoke burning in my throat. I bolted upright from the dream drenched in sweat. Propping myself up in bed I began to think about how much my life had changed over the past few months. I felt a bit afraid about what was to come. I guess the unknown is always scary.

As the sun rose I was beckoned by the comforting smell of coffee brewing and I sauntered out to Olivia's kitchen in my robe—bathrobe that is. I poured myself a cup and sat down in the breakfast room. A beam of sunlight streamed through the window warming me, calming me. I knew where I would go after my delivery in Paris—-the South of France. When I got to Paris I would ask the gypsy where the other relic was and go on an adventure.

I gathered my things together and headed home early, promising Olivia I'd be careful on this next adventure. I was feeling alive in a way that I'd not known before. Something was changing in me, something was shifting.

Damn, I had forgotten to tell Olivia about George Clooney.

CHAPTER NINE

The next few days were all about getting caught up again and preparing for the next trip. I was in a great mood when Mac called me. I'd not heard from him for almost a month, he caught me off guard.

"Molly, hey. Are you mad at me again?"

"Mad? No. Why would I be mad at you?"

"Haven't heard from you. No late-night calls. No need for any good lovin', huh?"

"I guess not," I said, chuckling at his lack of tact.

"How about dinner tonight?" he asked as if it was a last minute decision.

I thought for a moment. It was time for this meeting with Mac. I felt ready. I didn't know how it was going to turn out, but I knew it was right.

"Sure. What time and where?"

"I'll pick you up at seven. The Grove has a nice Greek place. The reviews are good."

"Sounds great."

Mac showed up right on time and it was actually really nice to see him. He looked so boyish and handsome in the navy blue birthday sweater vest that I knitted for him, or I should say my Aunt Sally knitted for him. I started it and she finished it. We didn't talk much in the car, I think we chatted about the weather or some other mundane subject. I felt the distance between us. It had to be me, Mac hadn't changed one bit.

They seated us outside at the restaurant and Mac took charge, ordering us ouzo and appetizers. Our conversation was all about his life—his stories and where he'd been. He went on and on about the two weeks he spent documenting the slaughter of rhinos in South Africa. The people he met. The food and wine he had. At this point, he had no clue about my life, nor did he seem curious. I wasn't certain I wanted to share anyway.

Everything that had happened in my life recently had been so profound, I felt very protective of it all. My experiences were precious to me. I didn't want anyone trampling on them. I had a purpose to my life now and no one was going to take it away with their skepticism. I decided to keep it all to myself. But when the waiter brought us the bottle of ouzo with the bright red number seven on the front, my jaw dropped. Even self-absorbed Mac noticed that my face had gone pale.

"So, babe, what's wrong here? You look like you just saw a ghost. Did I say something wrong?"

"No. I have a new job. I have a new life. See that seven?" I pointed to the bottle.

"Yes," he was trying to follow my conversation but seemed a little annoyed. "Of course I do."

"Well, that red seven is a message to me."

"Okaaay… and why don't you just tell me what this message is and who is giving it to you?"

"The message is that there are seven saints for seven sins and I have to find seven holy objects and bring them together again. God is giving me the message or maybe St. Anne," I whispered fighting back tears.

"Riiiiiight... you know, you never used to talk about religion. Are you feeling okay? What's all this sin stuff? It sounds weird to me. You'd better be careful talking to people like this. Maybe you need a vacation?"

"The universe is interactive. I didn't know that before. I thought it was absurd, but it's actually true. I'm learning to listen and I am hearing answers. I feel spiritual for the first time in my life. It's a good thing. A really good thing."

He held his two index fingers up at me in the shape of a cross. "Easy now. Do not go Jesus freak on me here, babe. Settle down a bit, you're making me uncomfortable. Maybe you need to see a shrink? Why don't you tell me about your job? What producer are you working for now? Let's talk about something that I can understand, you're a little crazyville right now. My sister has a great shrink." This was not all going as he'd expected and he looked absolutely bewildered.

"I am happy. This new job is just a vehicle for me to fulfill my life's purpose. Listen Mac, my whole life I have been celebrating other people's successes and though I've enjoyed doing it, inside I always wanted something for myself. When Olivia and I were in high school we made this deal with two of our friends that whoever made their first million would buy the other three a bottle of Crystal champagne. Do you know that I'm the only one who didn't make it? I realized one day that I was never going to, and even though my friends love me anyway, I've always had this feeling that it wasn't money that was going to bring me success. This is the first time in my whole life that I feel that I belong," I explained with tears in my eyes.

"Okay." He looked like a deer in the headlights. "We don't have to talk about your job either. Let's go see a movie."

Mac just didn't get it, I knew there was no use trying. I didn't feel angry at him, just grateful to have the verification.

"Can't. I fly out to Paris tomorrow and I'll be staying in France an extra week so I have to pack. Thanks, Mac, it has been really good seeing you." I leaned across the table right past the red seven and kissed him on each cheek.

He sat slightly stunned as I calmly gathered my coat and purse. I decided to walk home. It was a cool night, but I was dressed for it. It was over. Finally. Whatever filament had hummed between us, charged and kinetic as it once was, had gone dead. Maybe it is true that women find their divinity through the disappointment of the men in their lives. If I had been living happily ever after with Mac by my side, I would never have met St. Anne.

"It is all perfect."

Less than twenty-four hours later I was on the Rue de Bac once again. I stopped at the little chapel to kneel in front of the Virgin Mary. She seemed to be smiling at me.

An older lady sitting near me pointed to the statue of the virgin. "She love you," she said in stilted English, handing me a medal.

I felt blessed as I walked to the gate of my gypsy friend with my new medal still in my hand. Seeing me from the window, she yelled for me to wait. As if I had any choice. I waited and waited. This time, thirty minutes passed and I was starting to get cold. Just when I was about to leave, she unlocked the gate and hurried me inside. The room looked exactly the same as before, except this time she'd set up two metal folding chairs across from each other with a red pillar candle burning on a small table in-between.

"I make party for us!"

I had forgotten the shouting. It took me a moment to adjust.

"I see. Thank you."

"You get message?"

"What? Did you leave me a message? I'm sorry, I haven't checked my phone today."

"I no use phone. You understand?"

Oh. Yes, I guess I do because I am here, I thought as

I nodded my head.

"I wait two days now!"

"I guess I'm a little slow, but here I am."

"For you I have special price on everything."

"Thank you. I really only want the relic you told me about before," I said, remembering the honey.

"No relic here. I sell to dark man two days ago. Thanks be to God."

"Why did you do that? You knew I was coming. You knew I wanted it. I paid you cash for the robe!" I thought my heart was going to jump right out of my chest.

"He pay big money. I poor girl from Yugoslavia. What you want from me? I have mouths to feed."

I was speechless.

"You go South. My friend, she have special relic."

I collected myself, finally forming the words to respond. "Okay. Yes, I want to meet her. Tell me where and how to find her."

"How much you pay?"

There were the catlike eyes again. She was endlessly cunning, this gypsy.

"How much do you want?"

"Man pay fifty dollars for her name."

"What? You gave him her name too?"

"He no leave till Saturday. I give him part of name!"

"I'll pay you sixty dollars for the full name and address."

"Seventy-five dollars better price!" she argued.

"Fine, seventy-five dollars it is. Please give me all the information you can."

I wanted to get out of there before she changed her mind. I was actually prepared to go as high as two hundred dollars, so I was feeling pretty lucky.

She scribbled on a piece of paper, speaking as she wrote. "You go to town of Rennes-le-Chateau. Go to church and ask for Silvia Dupres—Silvia clean church. Tell Silvia you look for Astara. Astara have treasures."

I wanted an adventure and I certainly got one. But I wasn't the only one looking for relics. Now I had competition. Who was this man?

"Before I go, please tell me about the man who bought the relic. What does he look like? Do you know his name?"

"Big man. Dark man with big white teeth and black eyes. He wear hat. He come from Africa, that man." She held her arms high above her head to show me his height. From the looks of it, he was about seven feet tall.

I thanked her and headed back to the hotel. I was disappointed about the relic, it had not been there as I'd expected. But I felt something else deep down in my bones that was more alarming. Fear. There was someone else after the relics. Could he have found the note? I didn't have a good feeling about this man.

"You are always protected."

Hearing her words was easy, but trusting her would take me some time.

Arriving back at the hotel I glanced across the street and noticed a black man wearing a baseball cap sitting in a blue Renault Clio with no license plates. Thinking I must be paranoid I shook it off and went up to my room. I couldn't stop thinking about him so a few minutes later I found myself peeking out the window. The car was still there but no one was in it. Feeling anxious, I bolted the door and put on the TV to drown out my thoughts.

A little while later, someone knocked on my door. I almost jumped out of my skin. I didn't answer it and sat frozen with my hand on the telephone receiver, my heart pounding in my ears. They knocked one more time and I didn't move a muscle. When I thought they'd gone, I called down to the front desk. A woman answered.

"Did someone come to the hotel and ask for me?"

"No Madame Rose, are you expecting someone?"

"Did you see a black man in a baseball cap go through the hotel?"

"Madame, we have guests of all types staying here. I cannot say that I remember such a man."

In my mind I pictured the man with a gun forcing her to give those answers to me.

"Did anyone from the hotel come to my room a few minutes ago?"

"Let me check, just one moment, Madame."

I waited, trembling. It seemed like it took forever for her to come back on the line.

"Madame Rose, our housekeeper tells me she came to your room to give you a turn down service. Are you okay, Madame Rose?"

My body relaxed. I exhaled a long sigh quietly. "Yes, thank you. May I have a wakeup call at eight a.m. please?"

"Of course. Is there anything else I can do for you, Madame? Would you like your bed turned down?"

"No, merci."

How embarrassing! I was caught up in the middle of a Nancy Drew novel, but there is no way Nancy would have acted like such a scaredy cat. I took a warm bath and snuggled into a fluffy hotel robe. I was starving and ordered room service. Unlike my last job, I was losing weight on this one. Funny, I didn't even think about junk food any more.

The next morning I made all my train arrangements for the South of France. I couldn't help but check for the blue car. There it was, still parked across from the hotel. Sitting at an outside café for breakfast, I picked up a *London Herald* someone left behind on the table. The coffee stained travel section was all that was there. I opened it up to find an article on Mary Magdalene. It was an interesting article, but what really sparked my interest was the church they talked about. Mary Magdalene's church. It was the same church in the South of France that my little sly friend had given me directions to. I smiled. Tomorrow morning I would be on that train just one day ahead of my competition, if all went well.

Lost in my thoughts, someone touched my shoulder and I gasped. Looking down at me was an tall African American man wearing sunglasses and a hat.

"Madame? Sorry to frighten you," he said, his accent difficult to pinpoint. "You dropped this when you left your hotel." He handed me my passport.

"Thank you so much," I said, flustered. "I mean, merci."

"You must be careful when traveling abroad. To lose your passport is a serious concern, non?"

I thanked him again and offered him some money, which he politely declined. He bid me good day, strolled off and disappeared into a nearby building. Thank goodness he found it. How could I have been so careless? He left me with an uneasy feeling. Something wasn't quite right. Then it hit me, how could I have dropped my passport? I know I put it in the hotel safe when I arrived and I hadn't taken it out since. There was no way I could have dropped it. I decided to change hotels. Better yet, I'd take an earlier train.

I hurried back to the hotel and asked the young woman at the front desk for the train schedule. She offered to make all the arrangements for me, so I went to my room to pack. The first thing I checked was the safe, the door was wide open. I counted my cash, my traveler's checks—everything was there. I decided I wouldn't mention it to the hotel, I didn't have time for the drama right now. He had all my information, whoever he was. I focused on making haste, getting out of my hotel room as fast as I could.

I was packing my bags in a frenzy when I remembered the package. Oh my God! Where was the delivery package? I was on the verge of a total panic attack when I saw it sitting on the chair by my bed.

"Thank you, St. Anne!"

"Be at peace."

The phone rang. It was the front desk calling to tell me about the upcoming trains. "Madame have you considered going by air?"

"No small planes for me, thank you."

My family had a fear of small planes. We all had it. I must remember to ask my auntie why. Train it would be. The next train out was a sleeper. Sounded fun to me so I asked her to make the reservations. I'd have just enough time to make my delivery before I left.

The delivery went well. No Jim, no George Clooney, only Mr. Philippe Dubois this time. He was a very formal man. Behind his thick horn-rimmed glasses, his kind, gentle brown eyes endeared him to me. His presence was comforting.

"I'm heading to the South of France for a vacation," I announced proudly. Why did I say that? It just spilled out of me.

His eyes lit up. "You know, my brother Marcus lives in Eyzahut. It's a small village in the South of France. Please, let me call him so he can be your guide while you're visiting? I promise you'll enjoy him very much. And he's much more handsome than I am, Madame."

"Oh, it is so kind of you to offer, but I couldn't..." I rambled on and he interrupted.

"A beautiful young woman should not be traveling by herself. Marcus will entertain you. He needs to practice his English. Eyzahut is a very small but beautiful village. My family has a house there, you are welcome to stay there if you like. Please allow me this?" He smiled warmly.

"The cost of giving is receiving."

I agreed, feeling a huge sense of relief. This trip finally seemed to be coming together. I gave him my train information and he wrote down Marcus' number. As we said our good-byes, he assured me that Marcus would pick me up at the train station and be my humble servant.

CHAPTER TEN

Trains are such a great way to travel. A sleeper was something I had always wanted to try. My First Class berth was small but I had privacy. The conductor told me that dinner was served a few train cars away so I headed that direction. Once again, food had been forgotten, so by the time I made my way to the dining car I was ravenous.

Three professional soccer players were waiting for a table and asked if I wanted to be their fourth. I agreed. They were gorgeous, but had limited English skills. The only thing I knew about soccer, or football as they called it, was David Beckham. I had never watched a game but I read a lot of gossip magazines at my old job. Beckham's wife, Victoria was always in the tabloids. We shared two bottles of wine and they filled themselves up with carbs. I learned with some translation that they were all from Italy and a little younger than me. We had a blast sharing stories, communicating like a charades game at times to get past the language barrier. I hadn't laughed that hard in a long time.

Okay, so I ended up sharing my sleeper with Mario whose last name did not seem to register. I did have that brief moment of hesitation. You know, the "what the heck am I doing" moment? Oh my God he was so sexy! I couldn't resist his seductive eyes or the accent. It didn't matter what he said, it all sounded erotic. There wasn't much to speak about, so I let his hands do all the talking. We eventually fell asleep, our bodies entwined, until the swaying train car stopped.

There was a bit of awkwardness as we gathered our things in the morning but we kissed goodbye quickly as I made my way off the train. Amazing what a little loving can do for the spirit. It was exactly what I needed. I hadn't been touched or held in so long. Somehow it felt like I let go of whatever might have been left of Mac. Some kind of wonderful purge.

When I stepped off the train and saw Marcus holding my name up I almost tripped over my own feet. He was devastatingly handsome. Tall and tanned with dark hair and clear turquoise blue eyes, he was dressed in white Ralph Lauren pants and shirt with gold lapis cufflinks. He flashed a perfect white smile as he took my bags and I couldn't help but notice his muscular body as we walked to his black Peugeot. I had a hard time taking my eyes off him. Philippe Dubois was not wrong about his brother. His English was sexy with the French accent. I was in heaven. My bad relationship karma seemed to be over.

"Stay in your heart."

The views were breathtaking as we drove up into the mountains. Blankets of emerald green extending as far as the eye could see. Yellow, purple and red wildflowers were everywhere. There was still a little snow on a few of the peaks. I had to eventually open the window because the curvy roads made me queasy. The fresh air really helped.

We stopped at a small village en route for food. Marcus seemed to know everyone. Throughout the evening people stopped by to greet him and sometimes they would join us for a glass of wine. Everyone was so friendly, and of course there were plenty of those double kisses that I loved so much. I noticed the conversation kept coming back around to the subject of feminine power in the world. These people were passionate about their ideas. They had so much more depth than I was used to. One interesting couple spoke intently about male dominance over the female and how it was time for the female energy to rise and come into balance. They were very emphatic about the year 2012 and how it had changed the energy patterns of the earth.

A dark haired woman with deep-set eyes had been listening to our conversation from the table directly across from us. Before long she leaned in to speak to me. "You are not here on vacation," she whispered in my ear.

"Is it that obvious?"

"To me, yes. You are in a hurry and perhaps it is not what it appears to be. Do not look for the outer world to bring you what you wish. A gift came to you and there are more to come. What you think you are doing for the world you must first do for yourself. You must learn to forgive. It looks like it is time for you to begin this journey. You will go into a cave and find peace. Bless you. The second part of your journey is what you are really preparing for. Be wise."

"Thank you," I murmured quickly. I had the feeling she had looked into my soul and it creeped me out. I felt vulnerable and exposed. A big knot twisted in my stomach.

Marcus instantly noticed my change of mood, paid for dinner and politely helped me with my jacket as we left. Back in his car I relaxed, leaving the eerie encounter behind.

On the drive to Marcus' home in the village of Eyzahut we hardly spoke. It wasn't an uncomfortable silence, we were just both deep in our own thoughts. I started thinking about the church of Mary Magdalene.

It seemed like we were in the middle of nowhere and I was worried about how I'd get to the church in the morning. Interrupting the silence, I asked Marcus if he could take me.

"I've made plans for us in the morning, but I would be happy to drive you in the afternoon."

I stopped worrying and enjoyed the rest of the ride. We were both exhausted when we arrived at his house. He showed me to my room and I thanked him for being such a gracious host. Kiss kiss goodnight.

The next morning I woke up feeling a little anxious. Rolling over to get out of bed, I noticed the cards in their silk wrap on the bedside table. Curious. I didn't remember unpacking anything the night before. But then again, I was pretty tired. My cue to draw a card. I unwrapped the cards, shuffled and drew. *A dark haired man will help you.* That made sense. Marcus had dark hair.

I wandered downstairs to the kitchen where an exotic French girl in her early twenties greeted me, handing me a cup of coffee with milk. It tasted delicious. She motioned to a small room where there was a wonderful blazing fire in the fireplace. I sat down on a brown suede couch and wrapped myself in a furry blanket. She brought a tray of pastries, leaving it on the coffee table.

Enjoying the warmth of the fire, I was eating my third croissant when Marcus strolled in wearing a gray cashmere bathrobe. Sexy. I was tempted to rip the robe off but I behaved myself, saying good morning with a kiss kiss.

"I'm taking you to a special place this morning. You're going to love it. We'll have some lunch afterwards. A friend of mine is meeting us for lunch. He can't wait to talk to you about California."

The French seem to love California. I agreed of course, but I was anxious to get to the church. Marcus assured me that the church was on our agenda for the

LAURA BUSHNELL

day.

"Patience my dear one."

In an hour we are once again driving through the mountains. The winding roads made my stomach turn so I didn't talk much. I was very nauseous by the time we stopped at a small church. Marcus was telling me how he and his father helped restore the church years ago. At the time all I could think about was getting the hell out of the car but his next words stopped me cold.

"Eyzhut has only seven full time residents but many seasonal visitors. Restoring the church has brought many more visitors to our little town."

My mind stuck on the seven full time residents. Seven. Why was this number seven following me around?

"This church has a soul. It's hard to explain it, but I know it has a soul because I feel it. It was built in the nineteenth century over an older church, which was built in the twelfth century. During the twelfth century it was a Templar's church."

I knew nothing about the Templars but sensed it was important. Note to self: study up on the Templars. Thank goodness for the Internet.

A beautiful sister resplendent in full habit greeted us at the door with a big smile. She introduced herself to me as Sister Violette and kissed me on each cheek. Then she grabbed my hand, acting like I was her long lost school chum. I instantly liked her very much. She reminded me of someone. Maybe my Aunt Sally? Marcus followed as she guided me on a tour of the little church and its grounds. Her English was perfectly clear, I hung on her every word. The church was magical and I wanted to know everything about it.

At one point, Sister Violette asked Marcus if she and I could have a moment alone. He was happy to oblige, stepping outside for a cigarette. She motioned for me to follow her down some stairs to the basement. Underneath the church was a relic safe. Chills raced down my spine as touched the bones of St. Francis of Assisi and St. Dennis. Then she handed me a small pendant which she told me contained a hair of the Virgin Mary. Encased in a silver theca with the red seal behind the back plate, the hair was displayed in the shape of an M. My heart burned as I held it. I shared what I was experiencing with Sister Violette. Smiling, she nodded eagerly.

"Has Marcus seen these?" I asked her.

"No."

"Why me?"

"You are from Los Angeles."

"What do you mean, Sister?"

"The City of Angels, Molly."

"I forgot that the name Los Angeles means that. I'm not actually from Los Angeles. I grew up in Idaho."

"Many have forgotten, Sister Molly. It is perhaps your assignment to remind them. There is so much fear and pain in the cities."

"Do you think we all have an assignment?"

"Yes, I believe that Jesus has given us each a job to do."

"I am not religious, Sister Violette. I never went to church as a child."

"We all find our calling. The Church to me is my home. It suits me but I recognize that it does not suit everyone. I love the solitude it provides my soul. I am very content here in my home, serving the saints."

"I had a relic of St. Anne but I gave her to my best friend. I still hear her voice though."

"How generous of you. No greed there God! Did you find that giving is receiving, Molly?"

"Yes, Sister. I believe it now," I confessed.

"I have never seen a St. Anne relic but I know that they exist. Considerable portions of the relics were rumored to have been given to St. Anne's cousins, both named Mary. I have heard that they left the Middle East and came to Marseille, France—not far from here.

The relics were later distributed amongst many churches in France. St. Anne was said to be a very powerful woman. One of the oldest churches in Jerusalem bears her name. Oh, and since you like Anne you must travel one day to Canada. Of all the churches dedicated to St. Anne, none can claim as many miracles as the Basilica of St. Anne de Beaupre. I know that they have her wrist bone. One of my students is with that church, she writes me wondrous letters. Pope Leo XIII gave the wrist bone to Canada in 1892."

"Speaking of popes. Do you know anything about Pope Joan?"

"Oh yes. That is quite a mystery. I do believe that it happened, but it's something that is only whispered about. Women have always been kept out of the most important offices and somehow she, like Joan of Arc, pushed her way in. The stories are almost comical. The Vatican frowns on any such discussion. We must talk more later. Promise me you will stop by and see me again one day?"

"I will absolutely stop by. One more thing, Sister Violette, do you believe in reincarnation?"

"Oh, you are testing my faith, dear. It was part of our Church doctrines until the Council of Trent in Constantinople. I cannot imagine it not being the case because it just makes sense. Again, my home does not allow too much of this discussion but you must know that we have known each other before. When Marcus' brother, Philippe told me about you, I felt the burning of the heart. I have always felt guided by the Virgin. When I was a young girl I read Teilhard de Chardin's *Hymn to the Eternal Feminine* and I never forgot these words: *I am the single radiance by which all is aroused and within which it is vibrant. For the man who has found me, the door to all things stands open. I am the magnetic force of the universal presence and the ceaseless ripple of its smile."*

I was overwhelmed by this last hour with Sister Violette. We knelt down in front of the Virgin and she prayed the rosary. Profoundly moved as I listened to her recite the sacred ritual, I felt like I was immersed in love itself. My heart swelled with joy. It was all remarkably familiar and gave me great comfort. Marcus beeped his horn just as we were finishing.

"Please excuse me, Sister, I don't want to keep Marcus waiting. Thank you so much for sharing the relics with me and for talking to me so frankly, so honestly. This has been a true religious experience for me. I've longed for one. Now I know that what I've been experiencing is real."

Kiss kiss.

"Now you know."

CHAPTER ELEVEN

I was starving. Inside however, I had never felt so satisfied. I must read de Chardin, I thought. I could still hear Sister Violette saying, "The door to all things stands open." I knew I was supposed to hear those words, my visit with Sister Violette was no accident. I was dazed as I walked to the car. Marcus held the car door open for me.

"Molly? You look like you've been transported to another world. Ready to go?"

I nodded but my mind was elsewhere. As we were driving through the village, I noticed a blue Renault Clio parked just off the main road. Recalling the man in Paris, my body tensed. I suddenly felt a sense of urgency.

"Marcus, could we skip lunch and go straight to the church? I just need to get some information. I promise it won't take me long."

"Of course. Do you need my help? Molly, is something wrong?" Marcus didn't miss a thing.

I hadn't meant to alarm him and tried to put him at ease. The card told me he would help.

"Basically, I just need to meet a woman named Silvia who cleans the church. She's supposed to give me the name of a woman who I've promised to meet while I'm here."

"Well, let me help you. After all, your French is pretty bad."

He flashed that beautiful smile.

He was right. "You can definitely help me with that," I said chuckling. "I need to ask Silvia how to get hold of a woman named Astarte."

"Astarte Bilgio?" he asked, abruptly turning sour.

"I don't know. Who is she? I was never given her last name although I paid for it."

"It sounds like Astarte Bilgio. She has a small shop near here. I can't imagine why you'd want to see her, but I can take you there without going to the church."

Sister Violette's voice rang out in my ears again, "The door to all things stands open."

When we arrived at her shop I was deflated to see the sign in the window. Closed. Marcus noticed my dismal expression and softened.

"Don't worry, this is not unusual, Molly. Her store is hardly ever open. I was just hoping we would find her here. She's usually at the local bar. No problem, we'll find her there. Prepare yourself for a lot of cigarette smoke and an unruly crowd. They start early. If we are lucky we'll find her while she's still sober."

Marcus parked and we headed up the street on foot. There weren't many dwellings in the area. I couldn't imagine a bar being one of them, but I could hear the muffled voices of people and what sounded like music somewhere nearby. He motioned towards a shack that looked more like a run down barn than a gathering place. The voices got closer as we approached the door to find it cracked open.

Inside the dimly lit smoke-filled room I saw him. The dark man wearing a black knit cap and Ray Bans was sitting there alone. His focus was on a group of three women at a table nearby. I felt sure that Astarte was one of them. Marcus motioned to the redhead in the group and took my hand, leading me towards her. I tightened my grip. Aware of the dark man's eyes on me I turned away from his gaze. Marcus noticed my trepidation and put his arm around me. We sat down next to the ladies.

Marcus initiated the conversation, speaking to the redhead in French. He leaned over and told me that she didn't speak any English. They exchanged a few more words and then he asked me who'd sent me to her. I told him quickly about the gypsy, her friend in Paris on the Rue de Bac. He translated, whispering in Astarte's ear and she responded, suddenly very excited.

He then lowered his voice, leaning towards my ear. "Why her, Molly? I can help you find anything you want?"

"Marcus. I was sent to her to get something special. I don't know what it is yet," I whispered back.

"Madame?" The dark man was standing beside Astarte. He spoke to her quickly in French. She nodded her head, got up and followed him to a table on the other side of the room.

"Marcus, you need to stop him! He's after the same thing I am. Please!"

"Wait here."

He understood every word the dark man had said to Astarte and I think he was putting things together. He followed them and came back to me a few minutes later with a look of satisfaction.

Quickly leading me out of the bar he said, "Don't worry, Molly. She understands. She says to meet her tomorrow morning and she'll show you what she has. The man mentioned Sierra Leone, Africa. He didn't introduce himself. He's very sophisticated, but a very odd man. He wore those dark glasses the whole time so I never saw his eyes."

"It's so unfair! That man beats me every time. I hate that man!" I burst into tears of frustration.

Marcus put his arms around me until I stopped. He didn't ask any questions. He just held me, soothing me gently. "Now don't worry, Molly. We'll go there first thing tomorrow before Astarte heads to the bar and see what she has for you."

"I have to have this. You don't understand. It's not just for me. Please help me!"

"Of course I'll help you. I *am* helping you." He hugged me tightly and kissed me on the forehead.

"Now, let's go into Montelimar and have some lunch. Food will do wonders for you right about now. I want you to meet my friend. Relax and enjoy your vacation. This is a vacation, right?"

"Right." I remembered that even Nancy Drew always had fun on her adventures. Her friends would join her and they would go sailing or dancing. Even in the midst of a great mystery, she would always take time to dress up and enjoy herself.

When I met Jose I understood why Marcus was single. You would think that since I lived in California, my "gaydar" would have been spot on. I should have known. His fashionable clothing, perfect hair, buffed nails, flawless teeth… it all made sense now. How did I miss that one?

Despite my initial disappointment, we had an amazing time together. I really enjoyed the man that Marcus had been seeing for the last year. Jose was a beautiful man, his mother was Spanish and his father was Moroccan. It was a very sexy combination. The three of us had an immediate connection. They felt like family to me. The boys had all kinds of ideas about what I should see and do while I was there. Although it all sounded like fun, I couldn't stop thinking about Sister Violette and our conversation and the relics.

After lunch, Jose invited us to his home. They decided Marcus would leave his car so we could all ride together. Walking to Jose's Mercedes, I'd almost forgotten about Asparte when I saw the familiar blue

Renault parked in front of the café. I told Marcus I was sure it belonged to the dark man from the bar, briefly explaining how I'd seen him and the car before when I was in Paris.

"Don't worry about him, Molly. He seems to be watching you, so you must have all the power," Marcus declared.

That was an interesting way of looking at it. I had all the power. Maybe I did.

"Molly you do have the power and he's afraid of something. Tell us more about this mystery and let us help you," Jose chimed in.

It made sense really. Nancy always shared her mysteries. As we drove to Jose's home, I explained the whole story. They were intrigued and wanted to help me. Jose told me that years ago he'd studied to become a priest. It was expected of him as he came from a long line of priests, his mother's brother being a bishop. He eventually chose not to embrace the priesthood because he had serious concerns about the Church. He did this at great risk to his family relationships, but he felt passionate about his choice.

"The seven sins have taken over the Church, Molly. Over the years, the male energy has moved to the dark side. The universe has been screaming out for the feminine to return the balance. Now is the time for balance to be restored."

He surprised me with his candor and the depth of his convictions. And of course, his mention of the seven sins caught my attention. I needed to know more and finally had someone who could explain.

"What are the seven sins, Jose?"

"Pride, gluttony, envy, lust, anger, greed and sloth. Pride is excessive belief in one's own abilities. It has been called the sin from which all others arise. Envy is the desire for others' traits, status, abilities, or situations, something like jealousy. Gluttony is an inordinate desire to consume more than one requires.

Lust is an excessive craving for the pleasures of the body. Anger is manifested in the individual who spurns love and opts instead for fury. Greed is the desire for material wealth or gain, ignoring the realm of the spiritual. Sloth is the avoidance of physical or spiritual work."

"Have the male dominated churches just accepted the seven sins as a way of life?" I asked.

Jose felt they had. Marcus agreed. I was still spinning from the feeling of power I had suddenly owned.

We spent the rest of the afternoon and evening at Jose's home talking, eating cheese, crisp bread and drinking wine leaving the dark man behind us. We stayed up all night sharing stories. I'm not sure what time it was when I finally fell asleep on the couch. In the morning Jose made us coffee and omelets before we all headed out for Asparte's shop.

When we went out to the car, Jose noticed that the tire on the passenger side was completely flat. As they were pulling out the jack to change the tire, rain began pouring down out of nowhere. We were forced to run inside for cover.

"Do you feel you are getting stopped from this visit?" Marcus asked me.

"I don't know. Do you think dark forces are trying to stop me?"

Jose weighed in. "Sister, maybe the forces of light are stopping you because you don't need whatever Asparte has to sell you. That woman is notorious for her high prices. She has beautiful things, but she's full of pride."

I wondered if I too was full of pride. Many of those sins hit close to home. Marcus suggested that we all relax and let the weather pass.

All day the rain poured down. Even the earthy fresh smell of the rain wasn't enough to ease my anxiety. We all decided resting would be a good idea. I finally fell asleep to the patter of rain on the rooftop above me and had alternating dreams of Sister Violette and the dark man whom I had never officially met. He surely knew all about me by now. He'd probably copied my passport information. With the Internet, nothing was sacred. I could feel him around me. He was chasing me in my dream when Jose startled me awake.

"Molly, wake up. The rain stopped and we fixed the tire. Marcus and I have made a plan. We'll drive Marcus to his car, he wants to head home to take care of a few things. You and I will go on to the shop. We'll head up to his house after we're done and stay up there tonight. He wants to make dinner for us. You are in for a treat, he's a fantastic chef. Would you like to freshen up before we head out?"

"What time is it?" I asked, still a little out of it.

"Three p.m. Would you like a cup of coffee or tea perhaps?"

"No, thank you. Let me just brush my hair and wash my face. I'll be quick. I don't want to miss that woman this time."

Sometimes what we want and what we need are two different things. We dropped Marcus off at his car and made our way to the shop. No Asparte. We went from the shop to her house next door and then to the only bar in town. She was nowhere to be found. Something was standing in my way, preventing me from having whatever it was that she had. Whether it was the forces of dark or light I couldn't discern, but it was very clear I was being stopped.

When we arrived at Marcus' home the fire was roaring and hot drinks were waiting. A beautiful hand wrapped silver package with a blue bow sat on the table. A gift from Sister Violette to me. She'd stopped by earlier as she was on her way to a nearby hospital to take some relics for veneration.

"Another secret for you, Molly," the boys chorused.

I decided to wait to open the gift and read the note

when I retired, although it took every ounce of strength I had not to rip it open immediately.

Needless to say, dinner took forever. Although I enjoyed the conversation and the meal was delicious, I could not keep my eyes off the silver package. The boys were concerned about my reaction to not finding Asparte but I had let it go. That was a new one for me. Usually, I would mill over things, obsess and fret. After dinner I did the kiss kiss goodnight and left them chatting away together by the fire.

I carried the silver package upstairs. Once I was alone in my room, I carefully removed the delicate paper to find a little white box. Inside was a beautiful silver theca on a chain. The note read:

Dearest Sister Molly,

This is a first class relic of St Therese of Lisieux. A hair from her head. It was given to me when I first made my vows. It wants to be with you now. You have what the scriptures call "parrhesia"— boldness. Therese had it. She was called The Little Flower, and you are a flower too.

In the Love of Our Mother,
Sister Violette

I had my own saint with me now. Interesting that as soon as I let go of my expectations, I received exactly what I had wanted. Securing the chain around my neck, I knelt down and said a prayer of thanks. I felt the burning of my heart. From the corner of my eye, I thought I spotted a woman standing at the foot of my bed. But when I turned towards her, no one was there.

"Yes, you are blessed."

CHAPTER TWELVE

I could not keep my eyes off the relic that I was wearing. Number two saint was with me now. When my time in Eyzahut drew to an end, Marcus and Jose drove me to the train station. I felt a little sad to leave my new friends. We did the double kiss and promised to keep in touch. On the fast train to Paris, I sat by myself but felt as if someone was there with me. It was an odd feeling. At the airport, I went to use the restroom and felt someone walk in behind me. Again, there was no one in sight. St. Therese?

Olivia was there to greet me when I landed in Los Angeles. What a wonderful surprise! She knew my plans but I had no idea she'd be picking me up. Her eyes went straight to my necklace.

"And who might this little beauty be?" she asked, admiring the theca.

"St. Therese," I beamed, touching it for the millionth time.

Olivia opened her purse to reveal St. Anne.

"She wanted to come, Molly!"

"Of course she did!"

The four of us, if you count our little ladies, headed to my apartment. On the drive over, Olivia and I had a chance to catch up on all that had happened. I couldn't wait to learn about my new relic and who she was.

"So Master Catholic, tell me what you know about St. Therese."

"They call her the Little Flower. She was a Carmelite nun back in the late 1800's. The world came to know her through her autobiography called *A Story of a Soul*. I've always loved St. Therese. Arguably the greatest saint of the modern era she was and I guess still is very powerful."

"Speaking of power, let me tell you what I learned about power." I told her all about what happened with the dark man and how the boys felt I had the power. I was still telling the story as we arrived at my apartment. Opening the door, I felt relieved to find everything exactly as I'd left it. So good to be home safe.

"Those cards have been pretty accurate so far. I don't think you've seen the last of him Molly. Do you think you should move? You can afford more now."

"No. I can't take another change right now. I need something to stay the same. Oh, and guess what? I am not the mild dark woman. I met her though, in a café. She gave me a message, creeped me out a little at the time."

I took the cards out of my suitcase. "Why don't you shuffle them and we'll each pull a card... just for fun?"

Thrilled, Olivia grabbed the cards and shuffled like she was in Las Vegas. She chose a card: *Learn to rely on oneself for happiness and fulfillment.* She quickly put it down and handed the deck to me. Gently moving the cards around in my own version of a shuffle, I chose one from the bottom of the deck. It read: *Holiday – Get – Away.* The Vacation card.

My mind went to work in a flash, trying to make sense of it. My life was actually pretty exciting at this point. Why would I want a vacation? Maybe Olivia was a little jealous? She'd said nothing about her upcoming wedding. Usually Kevin called her every hour but her phone was oddly silent. Envy was no longer my friend. See how pride wormed its way in? Oh, how the mind can work sometimes.

"I seem to be haunted by the seven sins," I told her, sharing the conversation I'd had with Jose and his feelings about the Church.

"Some people feel it is better to take a more positive approach to faith and not dwell on sin. Others believe all sin is equally repugnant to God, and so any classification of sins is wrong. And then there are those who just want to forget the whole thing since they are saved and God loves them and really doesn't care about all this stuff," she explained.

"I've never really focused on sin. Not growing up in the Church, I didn't get that programming."

"I got all that programming and then some. Enough for the both of us, LOL! Okay, why don't we look at this another way? It seems the seven sins would each have a counter point. If you give up pride what do you have? Let's see... giving up pride would bring humility. The opposite of greed is generosity. What would be the opposite of envy?"

"I am not sure what the opposite is, but I think envy is a lack of love. Maybe the counterpoint is love? In fact, love could actually be the counterpoint for all of them," I concluded.

She looked thoughtful for a moment and agreed, but pressed on with her original reasoning. Olivia had grown up Catholic and raised her six younger brothers and sisters so she knew a lot about her Church.

"If one is content and kind then envy is not present. If anger could be turned to patience then lust could be healed by chastity and gluttony by temperance. What about sloth? That's such a funny word, why don't we replace it with another funny word: zeal!" She giggled.

"So there are seven sins that are plaguing mankind, everyone on the planet. And, there are seven sacred objects that need to be brought together and taken somewhere. Where they need to be taken is still a mystery. I wonder where this is all supposed to happen?" I pondered out loud.

"Any ideas?" Olivia asked.

"Not yet. Makes me anxious just thinking about it."

"Be at peace."

"Did you hear that?" I asked.

"Yes. She seems very present right now. I think things are really accelerating. Edgar Cayce, the most documented psychic of the twentieth century always emphasized the spiritual nature of humankind. In one of his books he says that because of the demands of life we frequently overlook the truest part of ourselves, which is our connection to spirit. Although we possess physical bodies and mental attitudes, ultimately our deepest connection is to our spiritual source. You are just more connected than the rest of us. I am so distracted most of the time but St. Anne helps me remember."

"Does St. Anne speak to you often?"

"Yes, she does. Not every day but often. Do you hear St. Therese in the same way?"

"No, she hasn't spoken to me. I feel her presence, as if she's standing beside me. Does that make sense? I can see her too. Not only in my mind's eye, I think I actually saw her standing at the foot of the bed a couple of nights ago."

"Wow! You're becoming clairvoyant."

"No way! You think? Well, maybe just a little."

"Would you like me to take St. Therese back with me for safekeeping?"

"No, but thank you for offering. I feel I'm supposed to wear her. She may guide me to the others."

"Do you feel that wearing her is safe?" she asked.

"Yes. Do you?"

"I don't. I'm concerned now that someone is watching you. Do you think this man is trying to do the same thing as you are with the relics or is he trying to stop you?" Her lips were tight with fear.

"My intuition. Listen to that, I'm using the word now! My intuition says that he's trying to stop me but I have nothing to go on. He feels like competition, but I'm not sure what we're competing for. I need St. Therese here with me, close to my heart. I'm going to wear her underneath my clothes so she'll be hidden from view."

"Okay. That sounds right. Good. Now, tell me what I can do to support you. How can I help? Are you hungry? Would you like to go out to eat somewhere?"

"Just having you here when I came home was exactly what I needed. Thank you. I really needed to see your face."

"I needed to see yours too. Want to get some new shoes?"

Leave it to Olivia to lighten the moment.

"Yes! Oh my God yes!"

Shoes had been our little ritual for years. Something we hadn't done for a few months. Off we went to Saks. We loved shoes. As soon as we entered the shoe department we were back on planet Earth. I found a pair of black Christian Louboutin heels with red soles. Heavenly! Olivia found four pairs, and then insisted that St. Anne wanted to buy St. Therese a pair of Gucci flats. Now that's my kind of divine intervention. Olivia says if the shoe fits, buy it!

CHAPTER THIRTEEN

A year ago I had promised my mother I would go to Idaho to represent our family on Aunt Sally's eightieth birthday. My trip from France was exhausting so I'd taken to my bed for the last couple of days. My place looked like a train wreck. Dirty dishes piled up, full garbage cans begging to be emptied, new shoes still in the bag sitting next to my suitcase that was bubbling over with dirty clothes. I'd picked out a few garments for dry cleaning which were strewn on the counter by the door. It was a disaster zone.

Everything I had done lately reminded me of one of the seven sins. I relived my sexual encounter on the train. Pure lust. It was fun, but ultimately not that satisfying because there wasn't a relationship or even the seed of something deeper. There was no sweetness in the kisses. I needed love. I wanted to meet someone, to get married and have children like my friends. Or did I? I always thought I did, but to be able to stay in bed for two days—that would never happen with a kid in tow. Probably not even with a husband. For just a few minutes I realized the perfection of my situation.

Aunt Sally had taken over caring for me when my mom first remarried. Mom changed husbands like some women change hairstyles. Mom raised me to be "the family". I was forced to be independent and alone while she was out socializing with her new friends. As a child I often felt that I was only an afterthought. Thank God for Aunt Sally, she was always available to me. It had been a year since I'd visited her, and then it was only for two days. I remember very little about that trip. In fact, I think I was so tired because of my job that I slept most of the time. My mom hadn't seen either one of us since she had moved to Budapest. Perhaps Idaho was the vacation the cards were trying to show me?

One week later I was on a plane landing in Idaho. It was a beautiful early summer's day, but as I drove out of the airport the stench of the pulp mill overwhelmed my senses. No wonder I never learned to breathe properly. Nothing felt right about this place. Aunt Sally lived about ninety miles away in a small farming town.

As I pulled up to Sally's ranch-style home on the outskirts of town she came running out to greet me. She looked about sixty-five at the most. Wow. Better than I remembered. It was a relief to see natural aging after living in Los Angeles. The lines on her face gave her a beautiful wise and soft look. We had a long hug and she made me a cup of hot chocolate. This was a tradition with us so I didn't have the heart to tell her that I hated hot chocolate.

While I nursed my cocoa, Sally asked me all about Hollywood. She wanted to know what movie and TV stars I had seen or met. She loved the stars so I told her about meeting George Clooney. Shaking her head she chastised me, her single niece, for not joining him for a drink. She was sure we'd be at his Italian villa right now if I'd only said yes to that drink. Next, I told her about Dr. Phil and his wife. I saw them at Madeo's, an old school Italian restaurant frequented by the rich and famous. Then I went on about the three couples who came up to me one night at another restaurant. They all thought I was a celebrity. They could not stop sneaking photos like paparazzi all evening. They told me as they were leaving that they watched me regularly on TV and really loved my movies. Sally loved that story because I heard her telling her neighbors about it the next morning.

A couple of days later over dinner Aunt Sally asked if I knew very much about my birth. It was a subject that had never been discussed, which I didn't realize until she started talking about it. I guess I'd never really asked any questions. For the first time I learned I had been born at a convent in Cottonwood, a few miles away. St. Gertrude's was a Benedictine Monastery, which still exists.

"Why was I born there?"

"It was the closest place when your mom went into labor."

That really surprised me. Maybe that was why the relic spoke to me? Maybe I was supposed to be Catholic and was taken away too soon? I put my hand on St. Therese, hidden safely beneath my blouse.

"You belong to all of life."

We decided to go there the next day and visit the Sisters. As we drove up to the property, a big red tail hawk that had been circling landed on a fence post. Auntie said it was a powerful omen.

I was discovering all kinds of interesting things on this trip. One was that I was pretty sure my auntie was a medicine woman and herbalist. Not only did she know all about the animals and the birds, I witnessed her doing a healing on a neighbor. Earlier that morning, a neighbor came by with a sick baby. Auntie gave her a brown liquid she had made with herbs and within minutes the baby stopped coughing.

One of the Sisters met us at the entrance to the chapel. She had joined the Benedictine Monastery when she was eighteen years old. Her innocent fifty-year-old face was full of light and love. She played the piano and sang for us a sweet song about her love for Jesus.

After the song she whispered, "I have something to show you."

Leaving the piano, she closed and locked the big doors of the chapel. As she turned and walked back towards the altar, I caught a glimpse of her eyes, twinkling like Christmas lights.

I couldn't help myself. "Do you have any relics?" I asked.

Suddenly animated, she opened up some big cupboards around the altar—full of relics! She noticed my reaction.

"I wish I could give you one, but you have come for something else. It has been waiting for you."

She moved to another area of the altar and opened a cabinet, pulling out a large bible-looking book. It was covered in faded pink leather with BE NOT FAITHLESS BUT BELIEVING embossed in gold on the front. The words were pale and flaking clearly due to age and use.

"This is what you've come for my child."

It was a book on the Virgin Mary. I felt the now familiar burning of my heart as she handed it to me, the sign I was beginning to recognize as being part of the gift. I carried my new book to one of the pews and started sobbing. I couldn't stop. I don't know what came over me. It was a deep profound cry. It took over my entire body. I didn't stop for a long time, I just kept crying. When I finally did stop Aunt Sally started, and then the Sister after that. We must have sat in that little church sobbing for about five hours. Overwhelmed with emotion, I had no choice but to feel it all. It was as if a dam broke and every pain I'd ever experienced in my life came forth.

Receiving the book was the last thing I expected when I came to Idaho. Now it seemed the mission had always been part of me, from the very beginning. I could have gone to St. Gertrude's so many times but I never did.

"I do remember your mom mentioning something about wanting to take you there once," Sally told me on the car ride home.

"I just wish Mom and I really knew one another. I want that connection with her so badly. Do you think it will ever be possible for us?"

"I hope so, sweetheart, but time will tell." The age-old prescription for whatever ails you.

The next day, I ordered a cake and went around the neighborhood inviting Auntie's friends to the party. It would be a surprise. Sally deserved a real party and we had one. I bought wine, cheese and crackers and made a big pot of spaghetti with too much garlic, her favorite. We all dined and danced and celebrated this wonderful woman. I had missed so many years, but this was a chance I could show her how much I loved her. I gifted her a bright green ski jacket to keep her warm in the cold Idaho winter. The neighbors said they could now spot her a mile away like a little lime in the distance. My mom called at the end of the evening and I even got on the phone and said hello.

A slightly overweight English woman in her mid seventies had been watching me as I spoke to my mother on the phone.

"If you met your mother at a cocktail party, would you invite her home for supper?" she asked when I hung up the phone.

"Good question. Yes, I probably would. She is very entertaining if she's not your mother."

"Give her a chance. She did the best she could. Do something nice for your mother. Not for her, Molly, but for you."

I almost relished in blaming my mom for all my problems. I couldn't help but feel abandoned. But maybe this woman was right. Maybe I did need to give her a chance.

I smiled gently at my aunt's neighbor and walked away to get another piece of cake.

The following morning Sally and I shared one last cup of cocoa before I headed back to Los Angeles. We chatted about my new job and I told her all about the gift. She was so excited for me, about everything. But then of course came the inevitable question.

"Molly, how is that young man you were seeing? Are you two still together?"

"No. It's over. Mac is all about Mac and we're not even close to being on the same wavelength."

Seeing the concern on her face I continued, "Don't worry, it's the best thing I could have done for myself. I feel really good about it, no hard feelings, you know?"

Her face softened and in that moment I thought of something.

"Sally, did you ever regret not marrying and having a family?"

"Not at all. I've had a full life with a lot of love in it. I loved my real estate profession. I met so many nice people and helped them find and finance their homes. I guess marriage was not my life lesson this time around. Are you afraid of being alone, Molly?"

The words fell like stones.

"Yes. I am."

I thought for a moment. I had not seen many happy couples. The only close couple I could even think of was an unconventional one. My neighbor, who was forty-one was living with her twenty-eight-year-old tennis pro boyfriend. They seemed happy. And she looked fantastic. All my other married friends were pretty unhappy. Olivia and Kevin seemed more like a business relationship. Being with someone had to be better than being alone, right?

"I want the fairytale fantasy. I want that man to ride up on a white horse and take me away to his castle. I want to be cherished. It is embarrassing sometimes, because everyone always asks me, why aren't you married? How am I supposed to answer that? Because I'm a total dud or because no one has chosen me?"

Sally contemplated for a moment before she responded to me.

"Molly, I understand how you feel. In my early years I was ashamed too. There was only one man for me—Bruce Riddle. He was the class president at my university. I went to the homecoming dance with him. He was not only handsome and intelligent but kind and sweet and so funny. But he fell head over heels for my best friend, Doreen. He said up until the day he died that I had given him the greatest gift of his life. They were married right after college and had two lovely children whom you know of course—my godchildren, John and Bruce Jr."

"I remember when Bruce Senior was ill, you moved in and helped Doreen with everything, even after he passed. It's amazing what you did. I had no idea you had been in love with Bruce once, and you stayed so close to Doreen all those years."

"Yes of course we did. I understood why he loved her. I loved her too. You see, she was the love of my life too."

"Aunt Sally! Are you telling me you're a lesbian?"

"I hate to put myself into a box. I loved a man and I've loved a woman. I felt different about them both, but somehow the same. Love is love."

"How did I not know this all these years? How did you keep it such a secret? In a small town like this?"

"We were discreet—which more people should be. We kept our private lives private. It seems easier for women. Your mom is the only one who knows. She walked in on us once and never would step back into my house, even after Doreen passed. She did not want to be called a lesbo. Oh, that woman… she's as closed as a safe at First National Bank during the evening hours!"

I laughed loudly in spite of myself.

"I always wondered why she wouldn't come here! I wish I'd been a fly on the wall. Do you know why she won't come see me?"

"She's scared to death of Los Angeles. Your father loved that city. You know what I think? I think you remind her of a combination of your Grandma Vera and me, with the frosting of your father."

"How so?"

"Your Grandma Vera was always curious about everything. She dragged us to every church in the Western Hemisphere. She knew everyone wherever we went and they were always visiting our home eating her homemade cinnamon rolls or she was mending a dress for someone. You know that saying, a cobbler's children never has shoes? That's what it was like for your mom. For me? I love to go barefoot! It's all in how you look at it."

Interesting. I guess I'd never been very curious about why my family was the way it was till now. My mom was never around to talk about our family.

"Your grandma was a mystic in the true sense of the word and she had powers in her hands too. That's where I got it. It is in your blood, girl."

"What do you mean?"

"Now, Molly, you can run but you cannot hide. Especially from me. I see that light behind your eyes. I recognized your soul as soon as you came out. You are destined for something. You have the bloodline. Someday you will understand that. Your father Hugh was a remarkable man. A priest of a man in the real sense. Part of the Masonic Lodge, and also high up in the Rosicrucians. He was named after Hugues de Payens, the first Grand Master of the Knights of Templar. Plus he was a descendant of the Grand Master of the Templars—Jacques De Molay. That's how you got your name. Your mom insisted on Molly instead of Molay. Your father had power that came straight from God. People gathered around him. They needed his healing energy. Not sure what he saw in your mom cause she was nothing but unhappy with everything he did. Have you ever read his poetry?"

"No. I had no idea he wrote poetry. I only have one photo of him when he graduated from high school. M-o-l-a-y. I like that. It's different. I went to a church in the South of France that was built by the Templars. Why does Mom keep this all so locked away?"

"Too painful I suppose. She kicked him out because he didn't have a 'real job'. She wanted a professional man and he was always changing jobs. Though he always managed to pay the rent she wanted more. He was in another world, lived in another realm or dimension. Everything he needed always came but in God's time, not your mom's. He was fine with that but she wasn't. She never felt safe with him. Your wise Grandma Vera always told her, "Trust in God, Margaret... trust in God."

Memories of the fights between my mother and father came flooding back to me.

"Yes. I remember the fighting."

"You must remember your mom yelling because I never heard your father raise his voice. I was over there a lot trying to make things right. He never had a chance loving her. Men are more forgiving than women. A little appreciation and they are back in the saddle. She was too damaged. I'll share something with you, Molly, and this is very private. When we were growing up, one of our neighbors molested your mother. Dad sat calmly in the next room. It happened multiple times. He knew about it and did nothing. She never forgave him. She never recovered."

I suddenly felt fiercely protective of my mom, shocked to hear this painful story about her.

"I don't blame her really. I am not sure I could be that forgiving."

"It is sometimes a life lesson to forgive."

"Life lesson. I like that. How do you find out what your life lessons are?"

"Well, I suppose you examine your life. Those that marry must learn about relationships. Those that do not must learn about freedom. I think there are many more women in the world now who are not here to learn about raising children. I'm in that group, although I love children. Something I've learned about myself is that I already know how to love them and how to raise them. I didn't have to have them to learn that. Over the years, I've watched my friends who had children and my gosh, they needed those children a whole heck of a lot more than those children needed them. What are my life lessons? I'm here to be free and to explore my spiritual gifts."

"Do you think that's why I'm here?"

"No idea, Molly. That is in your hands, not mine."

"It's all so confusing sometimes. I want both. Do you think that is possible?"

"Yes I certainly do. I think it is more possible now than when I was your age. You have more options than I did. There are more of you here. You just need to follow the path that your heart seeks out. Society did not know what to do with me. Out of two hundred in my graduation class I was the only one that did not get married."

"I want to be more like you. I want to be 'happy barefoot' instead of getting caught up in what I don't have. Sometimes I get depressed about it all. I think I'm just like my mom because I feel so negative and down a lot of the time. My friends are all in relationships now. Sometimes I don't even want to go out because I'm alone. Married people don't invite single women out often. Now that I am traveling, it's better for me. Sometimes I make up things about myself because I feel so boring. I say I do yoga when I never do, or I say I know a certain person when I've never met them. Stupid things. I know it's wrong, but I feel ashamed of myself as I am. Like I am not enough."

"We all feel shame, dear. But it does not become us and it is not who we are. We are part of God. That I know with my own heart."

"Love is all there is."

CHAPTER FOURTEEN

An avalanche of thoughts surged through me as I drove to the airport. I needed to get myself back in the Los Angeles headspace. You know, it's all about rush, rush, rush. Of course I was dressed for my return, wearing an Olivia-down. The purse I was carrying, the shoes on my feet, earrings and well, pretty much the whole outfit was all Olivia. She loved to tease me about it all, calling me her "little second hand rose".

Olivia spent her days getting massages, salt treatments, personalized yoga sessions, facials and the like. I was the plain friend who cared nothing for that high-maintenance stuff. Twice a year without fail, Olivia would come to Beverly Hills for the beauty visit, insisting we get our makeup done and buy all new cosmetics. She read all the magazines and always knew exactly what to buy. When we walked down the aisle at Neiman Marcus everyone knew her by name and now, me too. One day I went in on my own and they all started shouting my name, "Molly! Hi Molly! Where is Olivia? Is Olivia coming?"

Olivia was the rock star of the department stores. Despite her materialistic tendencies, she had a heart of gold. That is what I loved about her and I think that's what cemented our friendship. We were so different otherwise.

Home again, I slid off my shoes and settled on the couch to watch a rerun of *Modern Family*, my favorite TV program. I was laughing out loud when my phone rang. It was my mom wanting to know all about the family celebration. For the first time, I felt some compassion for her. It didn't last long though. As soon as she started to complain about my single status I could feel the old anger welling up inside me. I wanted to shout at her, ask her why she divorced my dad and why she yelled at both of us all the time. I ended up hanging up on her. Maybe I needed to see a therapist.

Instead of looking for a therapist I spent the next week catching up on household errands. I was tired of living like a pig. My good friend Lisa came over to organize me. Lisa was the queen of organization. The only time I had seen her house even a little cluttered was when she was dating someone younger. Now married to an older man she was back to her perfect house. Obviously bored she'd expanded her horizons to include organizing everyone else in the world. That was harsh, she was just trying to be a good friend. She came over at nine a.m. sharp two days in a row to help me clean up my mess. At one point, we were sorting through all my collections of hair products, cold remedies and cosmetics. Having a habit of saving hotel products, I now had quite the collection.

"What is this? Hotel Raphael. Paris, France? When did you go to Paris?"

"Oh. Last month. Actually twice," I said quickly.

"Last month? Are you kidding me? Where did you get the money to do that? Rich uncle die?" She grinned as she marveled at the fancy bottle. She thought I was kidding.

"I have a new job."

"I guess you must. I know your old boss Scrooge himself would not pay for the Hotel Raphael unless you were Cameron Diaz and had it in your contract. What's he doing without you? Remember the time he called you when we were at lunch? He was standing in line at the United counter at the airport asking you to call and ask for seat 2B. LOL! That man is helpless. Wait. What got into you? That's the dream Hollywood job, Molly. How are we going to watch the Academy movies early? Please tell me you're working for another producer? Damn."

I just got quiet. You can tell when people are asking and when they are just saying. She didn't really want to know and in fact did not mention it again. She went back to cleaning and organizing. Every once in awhile I would look over and she'd look at me, shaking her head. Eventually, she made one more attempt at holding on to the good life.

"No more premieres either?"

"No more premieres."

She left with very little conversation and I didn't hear from her the next morning. I guess we were done with our project now, at least she was. I had a few more drawers to sort through. I knew she loved me, she was just disappointed. The Hollywood life can be very seductive, but the reality of it is that it sucks the life out of you. I'm glad I got out, but I felt bad about letting down my friend.

"This too shall pass."

Anne's voice reminded me about the beautiful book I'd been given. I sat awhile and thumbed through it. Published in 1888, it had tissue thin pages, some with intricate gold etchings. According to the handwriting inside the front cover, it had once belonged to a James Riordan and was given to him by his mother. I fell asleep looking at the lithographs of the Virgin Mary inside.

When I finally woke up I realized I had a phone message from Madame's office. Frantically, I dialed the number, embarrassed that I'd missed her call in the middle of the afternoon while napping.

Blake informed me that I would be traveling to Budapest.

"The package you are delivering will come to you this evening via messenger. Your flight departs Friday morning. All instructions will be included in the package. Have a great trip Miss Rose."

Thanking him, I hung up the phone, dumbfounded. My new mysterious employer had decided against all odds to do business in Budapest. My mom just happened to live there. What were the chances? I couldn't go to Budapest and not stay with her. I reluctantly gave up my luxury hotel so I could stay with Mom and her husband. I had to call him Dr. Johnson. Not Bob or Dad, but Dr. Johnson. He was seriously uptight. I made the dreaded phone call to let them know. Thank God my mom was already sleeping.

"Hi, Dr. Johnson. Sorry to call so late, but I'll be flying to Budapest Friday for work and I was hoping I could stay with you and Mom for a few days."

"Well, Molly what a surprise! Your mom is sleeping. She will be so disappointed to have missed your call."

He asked for my flight information and insisted that Mom would pick me up at the airport. There was no use resisting. I told him I would email the flight info and said good night.

As I prepared for bed, I was still stunned over the trip I was about to take. It had been three years since I'd seen her. I felt bad about hanging up on her the other day. Why hadn't she told me about the things that had happened to her growing up? Sometimes I just felt so frustrated with her.

In light of the recent events in my life, it really didn't seem like a coincidence that I was suddenly being sent to Budapest, straight to my mom. I pulled out the cards, hoping for a little guidance. Shuffling them around in my hands, one fell to the floor. That must be my card. *Prepare for romance.* That was the best card so far. I fell asleep smiling.

I made myself sick on the plane ride thinking about seeing my mother. Consumed with my preparations for her questions and criticisms about my single status, my odd job, my weight and my living situation in Los Angeles—it took me by surprise when I first saw her. She was smaller and older than I remembered. Her hair was now completely silver. Three years was a long time. I wanted to hug her, but her dog was hanging from her neck across her chest in a baby carrier, like a shield. The little white fluff ball barked at me as if she knew I was there first and might try to usurp her. She'd had this dog for about two years, but I'd been very resistant to remembering its name. This despite the fact that any photo or phone call I received involved something about the dog.

"It's your sister, Chloe!" Mom laughed, as I snapped a photo.

This had to go on Instagram. Note to self: the dog's name is Chloe.

The drive to her house was quiet. I did not really know what to say and we'd already discussed the weather in Budapest, Los Angeles and finally even Idaho. I noticed her hand shaking on the steering wheel. She was nervous. I'd never seen my mom nervous.

Dr. Johnson and Mom lived in the Buda Hills area northwest of the capitol. It was a beautiful area for walking and cycling. Mom parked her car and suggested we go for a railway ride to get a view of the city. The entire railway was run by children. I loved it. The driver was the only adult on the train. I remember myself as a child singing, "I've been working on the railroad all the live long day!" I had never imagined that it could be true. We had an amazing view of all of Budapest.

"This city has changed me in so many ways. I have a lot to talk to you about," Mom murmured. She didn't say another word all the way home.

Now I had a reason to be nervous, as she gave me the warning but not the real talk. Why the warning? Why couldn't she just wait until she was actually ready to spit it out? Was she trying to make me anxious? She could be so dramatic sometimes.

But it was really difficult to take her seriously with that dog attached to her chest like a baby all day. She looked like a Miss America winner that could not put her trophy down. I had to keep from laughing every time I looked at them. Mom always preached that the word "dog" is "God" spelled backwards.

It came time to prepare for dinner, so I excused myself to shower and change. I put on a long black-belted dress. Elegant, I told myself. Another part of me thought of the black as a protection. Yes, I thought that was why the priests wore it. Or maybe I was just as dramatic as her? I cracked up thinking about it. I decided to wear a necklace Aunt Sally had given me a few years ago. She'd told me it was a very special family piece. This should make Mom happy, I mused as I fastened it around my neck.

I made an Olivia-style entrance for dinner. My mother's reaction to me was unexpected. When she saw me she actually dropped her glass of wine. The Baccarat crystal shattered on the tile floor, sending her maid Heidi running for the broom. Glass was everywhere, so I took the broom from Heidi and suggested she get the vacuum. As she scurried away to get the vacuum I caught a glimpse of myself in the mirror above the buffet. Funny. I looked like a witch in my black dress holding the broom. My mother stared at me, not saying a word. Then she pointed at my necklace.

"It belonged to your father's family. I have not seen it for so many years."

Just then, Dr. Johnson walked in the door, took one look at me and laughed. He couldn't hold it back and the more he tried, the harder he laughed. That got me tickled and I started laughing too. Mom was the only one not laughing. She looked like she'd seen a ghost. Intervening amidst the hilarity, she tried to stop Dr. Johnson from the biggest laugh of his life.

"Bob, Bob. It really is not that funny. What are you laughing at? That is the good crystal! Stop this!"

Breathless, I said, "Mom… it's me. He's laughing at me. It's funny. Look at me. I look like a witch who just flew in on her broomstick!"

This created more hysteria from Dr. Johnson who was nodding his head in agreement. He was now Bob to me. He was totally Bob. I might just really like this guy after all. I sat on the broom and started hamming it up. I danced with the broom like it was a ballroom partner. Mom finally sat down realizing she was not going to be able to stop anything. Bob poured some fresh wine for the three of us, and we sat, finally calming.

"So when did you fly in? I mean arrive?" He asked me with an evil grin.

"This afternoon Bob," I replied straight-faced, not wanting to upset my mom.

"Well you must have cast a spell on your mom because I have not seen her this somber for some time. Can you please remove it now?" He seemed to have missed the "Bob".

"Sure," I said, grabbing the broom to sweep the air around her feet.

"Bob, can you give me some time alone with Molly?"

"Yes of course, Margaret. Of course. I'll go into my study and watch the news. Tell me when you're ready for dinner."

"I will."

Bob winked at me and left the room. I sat, waiting

for the bomb to drop.

"Why did you wear that around your neck? What possessed you?" She was visibly upset now.

"Gosh. I didn't know it would cause this much of a problem. I just wanted to bring it for some reason. What is it? Why are you so upset?"

She took her time and then, launched. I had no idea it was going to be Nagasaki, an emotional atomic bomb.

"Your father had that around his neck when he died. I had to identify the body. I have not seen it since that day over thirty years ago. No one could figure out how it stayed on his body in the water."

"What do you mean water? I thought he died of a heart attack. You said natural causes."

"It was never published. Your father drowned."

"How could that be? Couldn't he swim? Why did you lie to me?" I felt the walls of the room closing in on me.

"Your father was actually an excellent swimmer. He went out into the ocean one day and never came back. His brother Charlie knows more about the details. He would not speak to me after it happened. Charlie watched him walk out and he never saw him come back."

"What brother, Mom? How come I did not know him all this time? I have an uncle? Who is this Charlie? I have no memory of him. Do you know what that means to me? I have felt like such an orphan!"

I thought of all the holidays I'd spent alone, craving a family connection. Rage erupted inside me and I instinctively touched St. Therese through my dress. I felt her hand on my shoulder, trying to calm me.

Mom struggled to explain. "When your dad and I separated, Charlie and your grandmother Mary took over. Your father was so vulnerable. He was powerful but weak at the same time. There was a pureness to him—an openness. Once he died, Charlie dropped out of sight. I heard he has a big company now. Your father was his keeper, his life. Charlie worshipped the ground he walked on. I was the evil one. I was the one that caused all this. His family never accepted me. He had to choose and he chose us… you and me. Oh Molly, I didn't kill him. I loved him with all my heart but I wasn't right for him."

She was sobbing now.

I wanted to comfort her but I was frozen. Caught between love and hate. Completely blindsided. My father drowned? I didn't swim at all and had been afraid of the water all my life, but never knew why. My mother hadn't ever noticed. She lived in her own little bubble. I would go to swim lessons in the park and run through the sprinklers to get wet before meeting my ride. No one told on me, but the result was that I couldn't swim.

"Please trust me! I tried to live with your dad, but I never knew when or what he was going to do next. I wasn't right for him. He needed someone who believed in God and I didn't. I'm only just now beginning to believe. I want to take you somewhere tomorrow. I've found my connection to God here."

She looked so pitiful, like a child who'd done something horrible and was trying to make everything better. I was still not talking and barely listening. I felt totally numb.

"Mom. I'm not hungry. I just need to go to bed now."

"Yes, Molly. Yes. Of course. I'm so sorry."

"Forgive her."

I went to my room and ran a bath. I felt like screaming. I felt so violated. I wanted to scream and scream and scream—but I didn't. I sat in the bath water until it got cold, then I added more hot water. I did this over and over again until my skin was all wrinkled and the hot water was gone. Imagining my mother trying to get hot water to wash her face gave me a certain amount of pleasure.

I dried off and climbed in bed and almost squashed Chloe. She had followed me into my room. Climbing on top of me, she sat on my chest and looked into my eyes. I felt a loving, comforting presence. I may have slept that way, I don't know. I just remember lying in bed going over and over what my mom had said feeling a terrible emptiness. Maybe my mom was right about dog and God.

The next morning my mother greeted me with a latte.

"I've become a barista!" she proclaimed as she led me over to her coffee machine.

She was acting like last night never happened. So like her. But her machine was impressive, and it was one of the best lattes I'd ever had. She sat down with me while Heidi made me a continental breakfast. Mom looked better today. Lighter, as if she'd been carrying this information for too long and now she had released it. I wished I felt better too.

"Molly. I wanted to tell you but you were so young when it happened and then our lives changed so much. You never asked me about it again. I was waiting for you to ask me."

"You were not waiting, Mother! You were too busy getting married to be waiting. You could have told me the truth a thousand times but you chose not to. Why? Why would you not be able to tell me about my dad? I wanted to know about him! Every time I asked you it was 'not now'. It was *never* a good time. God forbid one of your boyfriends found out about my dad or me!"

There was venom on my lips as I spoke.

"That is not true... that's just not true," she said trying to argue but quickly realized it wasn't going to change anything.

I had not reached that point yet. I wanted to fight. I wanted to hurt her. I wanted to blame her.

"Your father was an amazing man. Too good for me. It has only been since I came to Budapest that I realized how special he was. He believed in God so strongly that he died to prove something. He wanted to become one with God. He was beginning to understand the elements and was working with nature. Something went wrong. He was always so trusting and honestly I never saw him afraid. And he had plenty reason to have lots of fear. Instead, I was always afraid. Every day that I woke up when I was with him I was afraid. The moment I found out I was pregnant, I was afraid. Afraid that you would not be healthy, afraid that I would miscarry, afraid we would not be able to feed you and send you to college."

"I didn't even want to go to college," I said sheepishly. My heart was beginning to ache.

"I know. See, try as you may to control everything, it never works. Your dad did teach me that."

"Why didn't you teach me?"

"I'm not much of a teacher. You know that. I have communication problems and a small emotional memory, as Bob regularly points out."

"He's very funny. I've never seen that side of him. He must be good for you. You seem happier." I was softening.

"Yes. I am. I'm finding peace with my life, with my choices and with my God."

"I've never heard you talk so much about God."

"I never wanted to. I hated God. I don't anymore. I love you, Molly. I've always loved you. But I'm afraid I wasn't the best mother."

That was it. My heart melted. Whatever anger I'd been harboring—gone. My mom had not told me she loved me for years.

"Did I turn out that bad? I think you did a pretty decent job. I am a good person and guess what? I not only believe in God, I know God now."

"God is in everyone."

My mom smiled and walked over and held me. She then walked to the closet to retrieve a cardboard box that she laid on the table in front of me. She told me it held many special things for me. It had all belonged to her mother. In particular there was a purple rock crystal, an amethyst, which my dad had given to his new mother-in-law. Grandma Vera cherished it. The box was full of treasures, but today was the day I had to deliver my envelope, so I hesitantly put it in my bedroom to explore later.

Mom agreed to take me downtown for the delivery if we could go to her special place afterwards. It took a little while to finally get her out of the house as she was having a hard time deciding whether or not to wear the dog. In the end, Chloe stayed behind with Heidi. We drove to the city center to a business hotel. The delivery went well, except that the gentleman who picked it up was not Mr. Dubois, who I was looking forward to seeing. I was a bit disappointed. The quiet stranger handed me a pink bag with a beautiful little gold and white frog inside that I later learned was Herend Porcelain. There was also a little cloth sachet that contained some sort of spice. Back in the car, I showed the sachet to my mom.

"That's paprika, an essential ingredient in any Hungarian kitchen," she announced proudly.

Maybe I would actually learn to cook one day.

CHAPTER FIFTEEN

My mom was shape shifting before my eyes. When she met me at the airport she looked so old, tired and fragile. Now she looked radiant, like a young woman full of energy and life. I wondered if we all look that way, depending on what we carry around with us emotionally. She appeared to have crossed over dark waters.

We drove over the beautiful River Danube and headed up a hill.

"We are going to St. Ivan's," she told me.

We parked and got out of the car. As we walked, I could hear the most sublime chanting. A Gregorian chant that was pure and powerful, it also sounded strangely familiar. We walked through an entrance that led into a cave that had been turned into a tiny chapel. A few dark wooden chairs were lined up in front of a big cross with Jesus. There were several small caverns. Each had a statue of a different saint nestled against the rocks. White prayer candles and flowers of all types and colors were everywhere. We were the only people in the cave besides seven monks who were chanting.

We had entered a holy place and it was undeniable. Mom took my hand and we knelt on the ground together. I prayed that I could forgive my mother in all ways.

When the monks saw my mom they all smiled. Once the chant was finished they moved towards us, welcoming us. One of them introduced himself to me as Friar Jacques, and then kissed my mother on the cheek. He seemed overly excited to see her. If I didn't know better I would think my mother was having an affair with this monk. Even more surprising to me was that my mother spoke what appeared to be perfect Hungarian to him. She then switched to French with another one.

"They're going to pray for your travels, Molly," Mom translated.

"Thank you. Uh... merci!" I directed towards the monk she'd been speaking to.

He nodded, slightly bowing.

"Mom, did you tell them that I'm traveling?"

"Oh, they know all about you. I know them all very well. Beautiful people. Bob has been supporting their work for quite some time. He feels strongly about this church since it has helped me heal. This cave has become my sanctuary. All seven of them come to our home often for meals and prayer. Lovely evenings."

My mother was actually entertaining friars. I was totally shocked. When we left they all smiled at us. YNOT7? The memory of the license plate beckoned me back to my mission. Then I remembered the dark mysterious woman who gave me the message at dinner. She had mentioned a cave.

When we emerged back into the world I felt a sense of being reborn. My mother and I had been restored to innocence, free of something that neither one of us wanted. My heart was wide open and I was beaming.

"We have to go to the healing waters!" she exclaimed. "It's so lovely. I usually go to the one closest to home—Rudas Bath. Let's buy new swimsuits!"

All of a sudden I felt like I was with Olivia.

"Yes! That sounds fun." I couldn't believe my mom and I were actually having fun together.

We stopped at a small boutique and tried on dozens of swimsuits. The funny thing was, we walked out of the dressing rooms carrying the same suit. We were going to look like twins. Normally, I would have quickly picked out another one but something about it felt right. We were laughing like teenagers when we walked out carrying our bags. As we strolled to the car, a man with a white rabbit puppet stopped us. The rabbit puppet told us both how pretty we were and that we had beautiful skin. Blushing, we thanked the little rabbit for making our day. Mom looked so happy and relaxed, it really touched my heart to see her like this.

The spa had been operating since the fourteenth century. I had no idea of the Turkish influence here. The building had an octagonal structure and the main pool was lit by small octagonal holes carved in the domed ceiling. Sunbeams poured in through the holes, illuminating the pool below. I immersed myself in the warm water, it felt heavenly against my skin. Mom and I floated side by side, laughing and talking about our lives. We were connecting in a whole new way. I was moments away from telling her everything about my job and the relics when she made a move into old territory.

"Molly, dear, are you dating anyone special?"

"No."

"Do you want to?"

"Yes."

I suddenly wanted to take my matching suit off and wear something else.

Then she surprised me saying, "I wish sometimes that I was more like you. You are so independent and free."

"Really? You want to be more like me? I've never

had anyone say they want to be more like me."

"You're so pretty and full of adventure," she said as she held her two fingers up like a rabbit, "there is plenty of time to get married. As long as you are happy."

Oh—my—God! Self-improvement Mom had left the building. The angels were singing.

"Thanks, Mom. I needed that." I sank back into the soft warm water.

"We're going to go to one of my favorite restaurants tonight. Bob has invited a friend along. A lovely young doctor who is stationed here now. Bob says he could use some time with Americans. I hope that is okay with you?"

I knew it was too good to be true. Now I could see that they were probably doing a little matchmaking. My mother's urge for a grandchild could not have completely subsided. Maybe it was the water, but I felt content to just go with the flow.

When we left the baths it was dark outside. The moon was out, and the stars were exceptionally bright. I felt totally relaxed. We drove home chatting and laughing about the little rabbit. It had been a remarkable afternoon. We had such a wonderful time together.

Back at the house, I put on an Olivia-down and as I looked in the mirror I felt very pretty. I put my fingers up like the rabbit puppet and told myself how pretty I was and cracked myself up. It was nice to feel pretty. You know that feeling when you look in the mirror and you feel good about what you see? I hadn't had one of those moments in a long time. I added a little extra makeup, some glossy lipstick, and at the last minute put a gold barrette in my hair. I was prepared for romance. When I walked in to the living room, Bob looked surprised.

"You look fantastic!"

"Well thank you, Bob, you don't look so bad

yourself."

"You look gorgeous!" my mom cooed as she entered the room.

That was it. She didn't say anything else. Who were these people? Something had happened. Something had changed. Was it them or was it me? Whatever it was, I liked it. We drove to the restaurant chatting away. I suddenly felt like I had a real family. There was an ease and comfort level I didn't expect to have with mom and Dr.—I mean, Bob.

Waiting at our table was a handsome, tall East Indian man who introduced himself as Kamai Singh from San Francisco. Turns out he was a Ph.D. and an M.D. too. I found his big sexy black eyes quite irresistible. He was so proper all night, saying, "Miss Molly" this and "Miss Molly" that. We drank a lot of champagne and then had red wine with dinner. We were having a good old time in Budapest when Mom and Bob decided they wanted to go home. Mom said she was not feeling well. Kamai looked at me and winked. I smiled and shrugged. What could I do?

Kamai and I left the formal restaurant and walked side by side. Close. I liked him. He was one of the most interesting men I had ever met. Coming from a long family line of physicians, he'd trained at the Mayo Clinic, Yale, Harvard and Berkeley. He had over five hundred years of physicians in his family. He and his father were U.S. trained and practicing. Here I was, not having gone to college, strolling along with this encyclopedia of medical knowledge. Over six feet tall, he was in amazing physical shape. I felt a new confidence growing inside me as I walked beside him.

We took the underground and exited at Deak Station. Back on the street, Kamai led me to a little bar called Bar Domby. He said it reminded him of New York and he thought it was the best bar in Budapest. I guess others thought the same because it was packed. The crowd was chic but not pretentious and great music was playing. A vast array of colored bottles lined the walls behind the bar, all the best brands plus a lot of obscure labels. The place was a gem. The bartender Ankar was from Southern India and a new friend of Kamai's.

I went to the ladies' room so I could check my text messages.

Olivia: *Do you like ivory invitations?*
Me: *Yes. Perfect. Miss you.*

Lisa: *Can you get me into the new Johnny Depp premiere?*
Me: *No. Sorry.*

Marcus: *I had a visit from the guy who has been following you. He asked a lot of questions about you. I told him to get lost. Watch out Molly. Jose sends his love. We miss you!*
Me: *Thanks for your protection. I miss you both. xoxoM*

A knock on the bathroom door brought me out of my thoughts and back into the room. I unlocked the door and made my way back to the bar, where Kamai was standing guard over a seat for me. Such a gentleman. He and the bartender seemed at ease with each other as I joined them.

Leave it to a bartender to tell you all the secrets of a city. Ankar was built like an ox and very confident. Obviously Kamai told him a bit about me when I was in the ladies' room because shortly after we were introduced he told me I should go see his friend at the Ernst Gallery. He called me, "Miss Mol-ay". His accent made my name sound like the name my father wanted to call me after the Templar that was burned at the stake. I chuckled to myself at the synchronicities. The gallery felt important so I asked for directions. Ankar offered to take me the next day if I was free, which I was until about four p.m. My plane left at eight.

"Hey wait now, don't steal my American girl. I'm just getting to know her," Kamai teased.

"I know you, Kamai. Work, work, work. This beautiful lady needs to see some things in Pest," said Ankar, laughing.

The mood seemed to change after I wrote my mom's phone number and address on a napkin and handed it to Ankar. On the way back on the train I moved closer to Kamai. I wanted him to know I was interested in him and not in his friend. Moving away from me, he informed me he was married.

What? Why would my mom and Bob want me to meet him? Why would they introduce me to a married man?

"Does Bob know you're married?" I asked.

"I don't know that he does. You are a wonderful woman, Molly, don't take it personally. I have an arranged marriage. It is our family's custom. I am blessed as I am very much in love with my wife. She is also a doctor, so she was unable to come to Hungary with me. We have a three-year-old son."

What could I say? I felt very disappointed. Such a great guy. What was it with all these mixed messages?

When he walked me to my door I offered my hand as we said goodnight. But he gave me a hug instead, telling me he was so happy to have met me. He looked genuinely happy.

What was it with me? The ones I liked were either gay or married. Where were all the great single guys?

"Love is everywhere."

CHAPTER SIXTEEN

The next morning Mom and Bob were dying to hear about my evening with Kamai.

"It was very romantic. In fact, we're getting married."

My mom's eyes just about popped out of their sockets. "So, you do really like each other? I told Bob last night I had a feeling that Kamai is the one!"

"Yes. I think you're right. I just have to get him to divorce his wife and leave his child."

"What? What? Are you saying he's married? Bob, did you not ask the man if he was married?"

"No. I guess I didn't. He was not wearing a ring and he never mentioned it. I'm so sorry, Molly."

"Kamai is a very nice man and I did enjoy his company. I wish he was not married but he is and happily, I might add. No more match making you two." I waggled a finger at them. "On a brighter note, he did introduce me to his friend Ankar who's a bartender and has kindly offered to take me a few places this afternoon before I leave. He wants to show me around 'Pest'."

"Molly, a bartender? Surely you're not going to be interested in a bartender? Now let's be sensible. What kind of life can he offer you?"

Ah yes, the never-ending pursuit of a grandchild was always lurking. I found it sweet at this point. She just wanted me to be happy and well taken care of.

"I have a life. I'm not looking for a life. He's a very nice man. Now, I'm going to my room to pack my bags. Ankar is coming at noon to take me to lunch. Thank you for breakfast."

I kissed my mom on the forehead, she looked perplexed.

Carrying her little God with me, I went to my room. She sat on the bed as I packed my bag. I realized I was going to be sad leaving her. I unpacked the box of treasures and put everything into my suitcase. The purple crystal, a brown box with recipe cards and two small felt bags, a small statue of an oriental woman, a red pointed rock on a string and a tiny frame with a baby picture of me.

I sat on the bed for a long time holding Chloe, daydreaming about my father carrying my photo with him wherever he went. He probably never left home without it. I wondered if he had looked at it the day he went into the ocean.

"Be at peace."

"Anne. Anne are you here with me?" I felt the burning in my heart when I heard her voice.

"Always."

"Did you say something, Molly? Can I help you with anything?" Mom shouted into the room, breaking the spell.

"No. Thanks, Mom."

Ankar arrived right on time, all dressed up. He was a very handsome man. I had not really noticed it last night. My mom had a big smile on her face. She offered him some water or tea. All I wanted was to get out of there. He seemed to pick up on it and suggested we hurry so as not to miss our reservation.

"So Miss Mol-ay... you look very pretty today. Your

mother she seems very nice. You are a lucky girl to have such a nice mother."

"Yes. She's lovely."

"My mother died when I was a young boy. I envy you having such a mother."

"Oh Ankar, I'm sorry to hear that. I understand because I lost my father when I was young. I'm an only child and there is pressure, you know?"

"I am one of seven boys. My grandmother and grandfather lived with us. My Grandmother Tata was the only woman in our house of men. She was very tough on us. Do you mind if we stop at the antique shop before we go to lunch? My friends have such a fine shop, and they are not generally open on Sundays. As a special favor they have agreed to open their small shop for us. I do not want to keep them waiting."

"Of course. I'm not even hungry yet."

"What? Not hungry in Hungary?" he teased.

I giggled. He reached out and touched my arm. It felt electric.

"So Miss Mol-ay, here we are."

We had arrived at Ecclesia in what I learned was the fifth district. An older couple was waiting at the door for us. Laszlo and Krisztina had been selling religious paintings along with ecclesiastical objects for over forty-five years. They had some serious goodies. I found that out when I picked up a small box containing a nail from the cross of Jesus. I set it down carefully and followed them to a back room. Krisztina offered me some tea and a chair. Ankar was with Laszlo looking around the shop.

"What are you looking for, Molly?" she casually asked.

"Do you have any relics?"

She looked very serious and put her cup down.

"You are the second person that has asked me for relics in the last two days. There must be a growing interest in the United States?"

"I'm not sure."

I was now curious about who else was asking.

"The other person who asked you about the relics, what were they looking for?"

"Well, I have a few set out to show him tomorrow, but I suppose since you are here first we should show them to you. Does that sound agreeable?"

"Yes."

Oh my God, had I beaten him to something? It had to be him.

She called someone on the phone and then opened the large safe behind her desk. Carefully taking out a wooden tray, she turned and held it out to me like a box of chocolates.

There were three relics sitting on black velvet. I asked her not to tell me about them yet, I wanted to let them speak to me in their own special way. The one in the middle was glowing at me. Finely made of gold, inside was a small piece of pink painted paper carefully cut in the shape of a cross. On top of the paper was a tiny piece of bone. Again I felt the burning heat in my heart.

"What is it?" I asked, pointing to the one in the middle.

"Oh let's see... Number Twenty-Five. This one is special to us in Hungary because it is our St. Elizabeth, one of the Queen Saints. It is a first class relic—a bone. We do not know exactly where St. Elizabeth was born, but we know it happened in 1207. According to legend she always brought bread for beggars in her apron, against her husband's orders. One time her husband followed her and asked what was in her apron. Elizabeth asked for help from God and when she opened her apron there were only roses. After her husband's death she established a hospital where she nursed poor people. She was canonized in 1235. It comes with an authentication."

"What do you mean by first class relic?" I said as I

picked St. Elizabeth up.

"There are three classes of relics. First class is a portion of the body such as bone or hair. Second class is an item or piece of an item used by the saint. Third class is any object that is touched to a first or second class relic. I only deal in first and second class relics. They are the most precious and rarely entrusted to individuals."

She pointed to a small silver locket on the tray. "This little one is mother's milk from the Blessed Virgin Mary."

"What? Is that possible?" I was surprised.

"Well, dear. I do not have an authentic for that one. The milk relics never have them. Look at it this way. If it is real, you will feel something and whether it is all the prayer that has taken place with it or it is truly milk from her breast does not really matter."

"Yes. I guess that is true. Where did you find it?"

"It comes from Turkey. It was offered to me from a convent there that needed funds. I often buy my antiques from convents that are struggling to feed their sisters and pay their bills. This one comes from the Carmelites. They always have lovely relics. Some of the handiwork is extraordinary. Look at this one."

She handed me the third relic from the tray, a delicately embroidered piece inside a blue topaz encrusted gold case.

"This one is a bone of St. Paul. Very special. It hails from Italy."

"Thank you but how much is St. Elizabeth?" I asked, holding my breath.

"Interesting that you would choose that one. The gentleman seemed most interested in St. Elizabeth as well. He will be very disappointed, but Ankar is a dear friend. The price for that one is 1400 US dollars. I have promised Ankar that we would give you a special price which is thirty percent off."

"Okay. I want it," I said, handing her my credit

card.

Ankar popped in to check on me.

"Well, Miss Mol-ay, that is quite nice. I must tell you that when purchasing such items in Hungary, you need to know that all antiques more than fifty years old need a permit to leave the country. Permits can only be issued at the Cultural Inheritance Office. Permits could take four to six weeks. Why don't you let me take care of it and I can send it to you when it is approved?"

"What if it's not approved?" I frowned, anxious about this new complication.

"Well, I do not think that will happen. Being a bartender really pays off sometimes. One of my customers happens to be the head of the Cultural Inheritance Office, so I will call in a favor for you Miss Mol-ay. Oh, please give her back the credit card Krisztina. A good friend of mine wants to buy this for her as a sort of apology. Kamai called and when I told him I was bringing you here, he insisted on a gift. Don't worry Miss Mol-ay, he can afford it."

"It just doesn't feel right to me. It's too much. I cannot accept such an expensive gift."

"Well, I am afraid you will have to discuss it with him because I have my orders. You don't want to ruin my tips do you? I have to pay for graduate school. I am a hard-working bartender. Tips are everything Miss Mol-ay."

He mimicked a dagger to the heart and acted like he was dying. What an adorable man. How could I say no? The rest of the afternoon was magical. Everywhere we went Ankar knew people and they responded to him with such love. At the restaurant, he chose our food and wine and paid the bill when we were done. It was all delicious. I felt like a princess. He drove me all around the city, sharing funny anecdotes and charming descriptions. I was enjoying myself, but my mind was saying… *he's too short, too young, he's just a student, he's from a different culture...* but you know, my heart was telling me something different.

Ankar grew silent at one point. Finally he spoke. "Don't leave me now. Stay longer so we can get to know each other. Do you believe in destiny, Miss Molay?"

"Well, sometimes."

"Now?"

"I'm not sure what I believe right now. I am on a path of discovery. I am learning so much about myself and healing with my mom. I haven't had this much fun in a long time."

"That says a lot. Thank you for spending this time with me. I do not want you to go."

In the driveway of my mom's house he opened the car door for me and helped me out. Then he kissed me.

I saw myself in a pyramid with him. Only it was not him and I was not me. I was lying on a marble altar and he had an odd instrument with jewels on it. He was passing one hand over me while using the large crystal instrument in his other hand. I loved him and he loved me. It was so powerful that I started coughing uncontrollably.

I motioned for him to follow me inside. In the house I got some water and the coughing subsided.

"Ankar, I'm so sorry. That was powerful!"

"I know. I saw some images in my head that were quite remarkable. You were lying on a table and..."

I completed his sentence, "And you were healing me."

"Yes. Oh my God, you saw it too?"

"Yes. That's why I started coughing."

He held me in his arms and just then my mom walked in from the hallway.

"Oh, excuse me. Sorry."

"It's fine, Mom." I caught a smile on her face as she slipped away.

CHAPTER SEVENTEEN

On the drive to the airport I spilled my guts out to my mom while Chloe sat on my lap, mesmerized by my every word. I felt like a silly schoolgirl in love telling one my girlfriends all of my secrets. It was heartbreaking to leave my mom now that our relationship was finally evolving into what I had always wanted. I didn't want to leave her or her little God. When we pulled up to the curb, I kissed Chloe on top of her head and reluctantly left her on the front seat. Mom and I walked around to the back of the car to get my bags.

"Mom, I love you so much. This trip has changed my life," I said, hugging her tightly.

"I love you too baby girl. I'm sure going to miss you. It feels like we were just getting started. I'm so sorry for everything in the past. I hope you can find it in your heart to forgive me." She had tears streaming down her face.

"I love you and I forgive you. I hope you can forgive me too, Mom. I know I have played my own role in all of this too, and it has not been easy for you."

We were a puddle of tears when an airport security

officer pulled up behind us and beeped, motioning for us to move along. I hugged my mom one last time and kissed her on each cheek. Despite the tears, her face was radiant. She was happy.

On the flight home, Ankar filled my heart and mind. My seat partner was a petite Hispanic woman about my mom's age. She smiled and introduced herself as I took my seat next to her. We were sharing stories in no time. Pilar Strasberg had been in Budapest visiting her only son, and was now on her way home to Los Angeles. Her warm smile and gentle manner made me relax.

After telling me all about her trip, she began to open up about her son and her difficulty with him. It sounded like he had a lot of anger towards her. Unlike my mom, she had never divorced and was still married to his father whom she met when she was eighteen. I shared all about my relationship with my mom and how I felt we were beginning to heal. Pilar was born and raised in Mexico City. She had been studying the Kabalah because when she got married she'd converted to Judaism. She had also been studying many forms of meditation for years. When she said she could hear her guides, I thought I would fall out of my seat. I told her about St. Anne.

"That may surprise some people, but not me. I think it's more common than you might think. Maybe you were a child who listened to trees or fairies and heard their messages for you? Or, a toddler so in love with animals that stray cats and dogs followed you home, telling you their secrets? I know mothers who felt their child's presence before they were pregnant and actually called them in to be born. Maybe this frightens some people but it doesn't frighten me. You must follow this mission that you're on. I wish with all my heart that I knew what I was meant to do."

"I know I was supposed to meet you. You are a messenger and I really needed to hear what you just said. My entire life is changing and it makes me nervous. Sometimes I really like the change and sometimes I'm scared to death. Are you ever afraid?"

"I have been through more than a few dark nights. I have learned that fear is something to honor. I always say love is the gas pedal and fear is the brake. If you are driving down a steep hill, brakes could come in handy. Do you feel like you're driving down a steep hill?"

"Yes. I do and I've never had so much fun in my entire life."

"It seems to me that you are learning trust. Trust is the foundation all the rest of your abilities rely on. You must trust in the universe and the universe is inside of you. That's the real source of safety, not something from the outside. When you begin to feel the power of your prayers—the contact you make with the universe—then you have great wings to fly with. You just have to learn how to take off and land!" she said, laughing.

Her words seemed to meld from her heart to mine. She spoke with such kindness and generosity. I felt grateful to know her.

"Thank you, Pilar. I hope you find your path too."

"My path may to be to affirm people who have found their path. I don't know. Your path is very simple. Get out of your mind as soon as possible. All the tools you need are in your heart. Everything you need will be given to you and all you need to know will be revealed to you. Trust yourself and stay in your heart."

When we landed we hugged each other like old friends. Taking my phone number, she promised to call me and invite me to a women's group in Malibu that she hosted every month. It would be fun to meet some new friends and spend some more time with her. Pilar said there was a type of underground network of light workers that helped each other. That idea fascinated me. Could it be possible?

The next day I stayed in bed all morning, images of Ankar swirling happily through my mind. In my dream he rode up to me on a white horse. Finally, at noon I dragged myself out of bed and decided to check emails to see if I had one from Ankar. Nothing from him. Then, when I checked my phone I saw there was a text that must have come in when I was on the airplane.

My heart was pounding as I read the message.

> Ankar: *Thinking about you… missing you. I want to see you soon. Ankar.*
> Me: *I miss you too, so glad we met, come to Los Angeles!*

As soon as I hit send I felt a little scared at the thought of him actually showing up on my doorstep. How was this going to work? Why did he have to be so far away?

"What will be will be. Let go."

My plan was to go see Penny Anne but I wanted to unpack the treasures my mom had given me in Budapest. The little box with the recipe cards fell out and I felt the burning of my heart. Hmmm. Something was up so I opened the felt bags. The first one had a small pink crystal necklace in the shape of a heart on a silver chain. The second one had a breast milk relic exactly like the one Krisztina had shown me at her shop, only this one was a twenty-four karat gold locket with moonstones and pearls around the face. Where in the world did Grandma Vera find this? It had a very unique energy. A fourth saint had blessed my life. I put it on my bedside table and knelt on my knees in gratitude.

"The Mother blesses you sweet child."

Thanking St. Anne, I headed out to visit Penny Anne. I'd brought a gift back for her, plus I had so much to tell her. I dressed in some nice slacks and black pumps and drove over to Melrose, determined to turn down her inevitable drink offer. When I walked into the shop I was greeted by at least a dozen piñatas in various bright colors hanging from the ceiling. Several large Confederate flags had been strategically mounted next to antique mirrors, which made it seem like I was surrounded by flags. Penny Anne was standing behind the counter wearing a long, hot pink, embroidered dress with a sombrero perched on her head.

"Well, bless your heart! Hola, Molly! Welcome to my fiesta!"

"Penny Anne. You look festive. It's way past Cinco de Mayo and the Fourth of July has long passed, so what's going on?"

"Molly, darlin', I thought you'd forgotten your Southern girlfriend. How about a margarita? We have guacamole and chips too. We're having a lovely fiesta today. My sweet mama would have liked this fiesta almost as much as her festivities on April twenty-sixth. Sweetheart, it's not proper to wear black shoes till after Labor Day you should have worn white pumps. But I do love your attire, and your skin is so dewy. Why, you are glowing, darlin'. Are you in love?"

"Yes! I met the most amazing man in Budapest. I'm just a little uncertain because he's a bartender right now, but he's going to graduate school. I don't even know what he's studying. But when we kissed... oh... Penny Anne! It was the most amazing kiss I have ever had. But now that I am back I feel a little down because he's so far away. I can't stop thinking about him."

"Well of course you can't honey, nor should you! You are ripe for the picking, girl, I've been noticing it for a while now. Nothing like a little electricity to put some color on your cheeks."

"I brought you some pálinka. It's kind of like a brandy, I think. From Budapest. I hope you like it."

"I just adore palinka. It's distilled from fruit so I am sure it is healthy. Ah yes, forty percent alcohol. It's a strong spirit. Bless your heart. Now, we must share a drink."

"There you go," she said presenting an icy cold margarita out of nowhere.

"My, your hair could sure use some product, Molly, and I know you could have taken just a little more time preparing for my party. You should always look your best even if you feel your worst. It may not be April twenty-sixth but it is an important day."

"For the record, Penny Anne, I did not know you were having a fiesta today and what is so important about April twenty-sixth? I've never heard of it."

"April twenty-sixth is the Confederate Memorial Day, a very important holiday to us Southern folk. On this day we celebrate our heritage and remember those of our ancestors who gave their lives so that our beloved Southland would be free. The South is going to rise again!"

"Well, why are you celebrating today? It's the end of July."

"Oh cucaracha! I neglected to inform you of the treasures I have procured. It is a day to be remembered. While I was south of the border, I was offered the opportunity of a lifetime. A very prosperous client of mine needed to sell some of his collection. His shipping business has taken a turn for the worse, poor thing. His collection of thirteenth century French furniture and curios is out of this world. I was able to take a few pieces off his hands at a very good price. If I want to overpay I'll go to Neiman Marcus," she winked.

"Well, they all arrived today so you're just in time to help me unpack the crate, missy! Enjoy your libation first and then if you could give a lady a hand, it would be most appreciated. The furniture had once belonged to an aristocratic family in Rouen, France, the

Normandy area of France. Most of the pieces that I bought belonged originally to the Canon of the church of that day."

She handed me a photograph of an elaborate piece of furniture, like nothing I'd ever seen.

"Will you look at this? Molly, darlin', I have purchased this very tabernacle. Now let's unpack it."

We opened the wooden crate that was bursting with a confetti of styrofoam for padding. I tried to control the little pieces as they popped out like popcorn, with very little success. She lifted out the enamel piece and checked every inch of it to be sure there were no chips, as it was Limoges circa 1250.

"Will you sell it? Is this copper?" I asked opening a small drawer.

A pocket-sized object wrapped in blue velvet fell out of the drawer. Penny Anne picked it up and removed the velvet. Inside was a silver theca.

"Molly, I think you have another gift coming! Here is another one of those little things you like so much. I don't have a use for it, darlin', so it might as well go home with you. Please tell whoever it is that it should not be wearing velvet after February. That is just bad manners."

"Penny Anne, thank you so much. It must be one of the saints I'm supposed to bring together to heal the seven sins."

"Well, sugar, I have no idea what you are talkin' about but are you sure there are seven? I only know four: bad hair, bad manners, bad blind dates and bad dancers."

I was laughing as I turned the relic over in my hands. Inside the theca was a small piece of fabric and I could make out something written in small script: St. Jeanne. As I held it I felt the warmth building in my heart. This was meant to be. I recalled my conversation with Olivia about Joan of Arc and Mark Twain's book.

Penny Anne was not interested in Joan—she was

uncrating many other treasures. Then he walked in. A tanned and exceptionally handsome man appeared from the back room holding two margaritas. Wearing a white straw hat, white shirt and pants and white sandals, he was at least thirty years younger than Penny Anne. We introduced ourselves as he handed me a drink.

"Hello, Molly. I've heard so much about you. I'm Trey," he said with an Australian accent.

Penny Anne scored with this one! He oozed sexuality.

"How do you like our treasures?"

"Quite remarkable."

"Molly, show him your gift," Penny Anne chimed in.

I took the relic out of the velvet and handed it to him. He examined it carefully for a moment. He looked stunned.

"St. Jeanne. Bloody hell, this is a relic of Joan of Arc! This is extremely rare. We must take it to Sotheby's and have it examined for authenticity. This could be the find of the century. Bloody hell, Penny Anne, we may have found gold here!"

I wasn't sure how to react. I felt my hands grabbing her back. She was mine now but I didn't know what to say or do. She was part of my future. She was supposed to be with me. The thoughts were racing through my head.

"Let go."

St. Anne? I excused myself and went in the bathroom.

"St. Anne? Please help me."

"To have give all to all."

"What does that mean?"

Confused, I went back out and could hear an argument going on.

"You are a foolish woman, Penny Anne." Trey got quiet as soon as he saw me.

Penny Anne was very uncomfortable. I could tell she was upset.

"Look, Penny Anne. You don't have to give this to me. Keep her. I mean—it."

"No. No. You take her home. Possession is nine tenths of the law. I'm not an Indian giver. Southern girls know men may come and go, but girlfriends are fo'evah."

I departed with St. Joan of Arc feeling like I'd left a fire behind me. She was brave, she could handle this, I reconciled with myself. On the way home I dialed as I drove.

"Olivia. God, you will not believe what just happened!"

"Try me."

"I have just left the antique shop on Melrose. I helped Penny Anne unpack a crate. She bought an amazing thirteenth century piece, a Limoges tabernacle originally from Normandy. Inside one of the drawers was a relic of St. Jeanne. I think it's a relic of Joan of Arc."

"No way! There is only one known to exist. It's not possible. I think you should bring her here right away and that book too. I want to see everything. Joan of Arc was burned at the stake in the Normandy area. You're getting close to finding all seven, Molly."

"There's a slight problem. Penny Anne gave it to me but her boyfriend or husband—whatever he is—saw it and thinks it is valuable. He wanted her to take it for appraisal but she told him she gave it to me. He got really upset. She told me to take it, but it was really awkward. They're fighting now."

"Did you offer it back?"

"Yes, of course, first thing. But she insisted."

"Well then it must be for you."

"I don't have a great feeling about this. Somehow I doubt that is the case here."

"Don't let them take your gift away."

"Ok you are right I won't let them take the gift away."

"Bring it to Laguna. When can you come?"

"I'm not sure yet. Why don't I... Oh, Penny Anne is calling. I'll call you back."

I hung up with Olivia and switched over to Penny Anne.

"Hello?"

"Molly dear, it's Penny Anne. Well, Trey and I feel that we need to get this little thing checked out. You have already been given one gift, perhaps two is just one too many. Let's slow down here and get it appraised and of course you'll get the first chance to purchase it. I know it might not be fair but if life were fair, pecan pie would have no calories. If you could just drop it by when you can. We'll find out more about it and go from there, okay, honey?"

She was a steel magnolia so I knew Trey had really pushed her into this. She didn't sound like herself.

"Penny Anne, it sounds like you're unsure about this. I can understand that. If you want the gift back then you are going against everything you've already told me today. I feel that I'm supposed to have it. Are you sure about all of this?"

"I feel about as sweet as vinegar pie right now."

"I get that. I'll do whatever you wish. Why don't you just let me hold on to it over the weekend so I can enjoy it? It will give us both time to think and Monday morning we can talk about it. Okay?"

"That sounds perfect." She sounded relieved.

Not having the energy to travel to Olivia's, I spent the weekend looking up things online. I learned a lot about the Templars, the Mayan Prophecy and so many other things. I got lost in cyberspace.

Monday morning came and I hadn't heard from Penny Anne so I drove to the shop. Closed. It was past eleven a.m. This was not normal. Where was my spirit-loving gal? Just as I was driving away, I spotted her going in the back door so I reparked.

Peering through the front door I saw how sad she was. Talking on the phone, she was blowing her nose and wiping her eyes. It felt too private to witness. I drove away with St. Joan in my handbag.

What to do? It was hard to see Penny Anne so unhappy. I decided to go home and regroup. I would dress myself up, put on some makeup, do my hair and go back with a bottle of champagne. Remember the honey.

When I walked into the antique store Penny Anne looked fresh.

"Well butter my biscuit aren't you a sight for sore eyes! Look at how breathtaking you look. St. Joan must agree with you. Now darlin' I think that bottle of bubbly is exactly what we need. I let my mouth overload my tail, darlin'. I've had enough husbands now to know that you don't let the tail wag the dog. Trey was getting too big for his britches and well, shut my mouth. You are I are not going to piddle our time away over him. So let's celebrate, missy!"

I opened the bottle and poured the bubbly into her two tall crystal flutes.

"Now, honey, this is how I like to mend fences."

"There are no fences to mend, Penny Anne. By the way, you look beautiful."

"Well nothing like a good cry to make you look better. I swear it's the fountain of youth. It takes salt water out of the body and puts it back into the ocean of life. And of course, it leaves a lot more room for this!" She held up her glass victoriously.

"How long have you been married to Trey?"

"Oh, honey. We're not married. He was just what you might call a 'boy toy'. I was so down and out after my sixth husband died that I was like a possum. He woke me right up. But I cannot continue to carry on this foolishness when he is just after my money. You know the sun don't shine on the same dog's tail all the time."

"What are you saying?" I said, laughing.

"He'll get what he deserves!"

"And you will too. Next time we have to have the Green Goddamn. Whatever that drink is."

"It's a promise, missy."

I drove away from the antique shop with St. Joan on the passenger seat and a small yellowed envelope that she handed me as I left. Inside was an authentic. My new treasure was a second class relic of St. Joan. A piece of fabric from behind her armor. I suddenly felt brave enough to complete this mission.

CHAPTER EIGHTEEN

I had the dream again.

I was walking among the tall buildings of a city when I began to fly. That wasn't unusual for me, flying. But in this dream, as I looked down at the sidewalk, I realized that the dark man had seen me—and no one had ever seen me fly. It's not that I was invisible when I flew. But maybe people, even in dreams, can't see what they don't expect. He saw me though. He looked up and caught my eye. Alarmed, I flew away fast over buildings and parks and homes and freeways. I flew for miles and landed near a river, breathless.

"Hello, Molly." He stood over me, smiling.

I shuddered at his cold and empty eyes. He glanced at my feet. I followed his gaze to discover I was wearing glittering red sequined shoes, like the ruby slippers in *The Wizard of Oz*. The scarf around his neck turned into a huge white snake, hissing at me. Terrified, once more I flew away. At the end of the dream I was at an airport where they were checking people's IDs against a wanted poster with my face on it. I was trying to sneak on to a plane when I woke up. Drenched in sweat and shaken, I sat up in bed.

When the phone rang at seven a.m. it startled me. It was Olivia on her way to Los Angeles for a board meeting. She needed to get her hair done so I told her I'd meet up with her at the salon. Someone had to take care of St. Anne while Olivia got her hair colored. Olivia would use any excuse to have company, she loved having an entourage. That night we all stayed at the Beverly Hills Hotel.

I was awakened in the middle of the night by a glimmering ball of blue light. As the ball came near me it evolved into an angel and spread its wings over me. I could feel it permeate my entire body. Every cell was vibrating and I felt that I could not move if I wanted to. I was frozen in place. Was it a dream? I told Olivia all about it when we woke up the next morning.

She shot up in bed. "I saw it! I saw the blue light come into the room and move towards you. I closed my eyes and I saw it and I opened my eyes and I still saw it! That was not a dream Molly, it really happened. I saw it with my own two eyes!"

So it was real. How could both of us make up the same story? Instead of being a comfort, Olivia actually seeing my dream created more anxiety for me. The reality that I thought was real was no longer making sense and this new world seemed more and more liquid and somehow unformed. I had no one besides Olivia to really talk to. My new friend, Pilar would have been perfect to share all of this with. She had not called and I hadn't taken her number. I felt lost. Olivia had always hoped for these experiences, but I knew she couldn't guide me. She was out of her league here. Besides, she had her wedding to think about. All of my other friends were happily living in the world of jobs, relationships, money and movies. None of that world made much sense to me anymore.

After Olivia left for home I became very depressed. All these strange things were scaring me. In fact, I started feeling very uncomfortable with the changes that were happening in my life. One day I thought of a friend out the blue and she called me. The next day I woke up thinking about green glass and a neighbor brought me a bouquet of flowers in a green vase. I was not only hearing things, I was beginning to see things. I swear a woman was standing in my bedroom one night. The next morning, I picked up my miraculous medal from the bedside table and it burned my hand!

A week passed. I sank deeper into depression, spending my days in bed, lifeless and alone. I would not leave my apartment. Madame's office called but I told Blake I was sick. Ankar sent texts and emails that I couldn't even read. I spoke out loud to St. Anne and she never spoke back. I called on St. Therese and nothing happened. I took out the Mary book and read, hoping for clarity. None came. Even my newest relic offered no hope. St. Joan just sat there on my bedside table silent and still. Finally, as a last resort I decided to pull a card from the deck. The Death card: *It is a time of rebirth.*

The second week, Aunt Sally called to say hello. When she discovered the state I was in, she decided that she was coming to see me. She'd take the bus because she didn't want to fly anymore. She said we St. Claires needed to keep our feet on the ground.

"Mom is a St. Claire and she flies and I'm a Rose Aunt Sally," I reminded her.

I had not even thought about my mom's last name because she'd changed it so many times. I guess I had grown up with a saint.

A few days later, Sally arrived at my apartment on a mission. Unpacking her suitcase, she removed a big drum made of bear hide, an eagle feather, some sage and a deerskin bag filled with herbs. She proudly announced that she had brought her "medicine" to heal my feminine spirit. My feeble attempts to dissuade her fell on deaf ears.

Sally started drumming and declared she was going

to lead me on a journey to meet my power animal. She shook a rattle and spoke in a singsong voice. Despite my initial resistance, I eventually drifted into the ocean where I found myself face to face with a whale. She asked me what I saw and I told her—a whale. Convinced that I was to meet a mountain lion, she took me back in. She led me deep into the forest, then underneath the rich soil of the earth and finally, high up into the mountains. Each time, I found myself slipping into the ocean again. It was no use. She said I wasn't ready to walk on the earth with her medicine, explaining that what I was experiencing was an ego death—or dark night of the soul. Whatever it was, it made me feel worse, not better. Those damn cards always seemed to be right.

After the third day of drumming, the man downstairs came up and asked us to stop the racket and the stomping. I was relieved. It was becoming too much. I was tired of all the "medicine". All I could do was rest and cry for days after that.

Auntie baked me muffins and put smiles on my eggs each morning hoping I would pass through the dark night. She lay in bed with me at night and whispered to me about how it would all pass. She made herbal concoctions that seemed to slowly help. She threatened to bring the drum out again as soon as I felt better. She didn't give a darn about the downstairs neighbor.

Another week passed like this. Then one afternoon after a warm saltwater bath Sally had insisted on, I was sitting up in bed for the first time in days. She casually strolled in with a sneaky grin on her face... definitely up to something. She handed me a dark brown leather notebook. It was weathered and barely held together at the seams by red threads. There were papers crammed inside, bursting to get out.

"Your birthday is coming up. I wanted to give this to you early. Happy birthday Molly! This diary belonged to your dad. I found it a few weeks ago when I was cleaning out the barn. There's a whole box of things he brought over before he died. You can see everything later but this wanted to come to you now."

I had completely forgotten my upcoming birthday.

"Did it speak to you, Sally? Did you hear a voice?" I asked, struggling for some sanity.

"It was a nudge, girl. It just wanted to come and I knew it."

I began to cry as I held this little part of my father. I ran my fingers up and down the seams and over the leather. Auntie brought me a cup of herbal tea and quietly left the room. It was in my favorite blue-flowered china cup. A cup from my childhood, one of the few things I had kept.

Opening the book I noticed his name, *Hugh Rose* was handwritten inside the cover. I had never seen his handwriting. My father's diary. It gave me such a feeling of peace. I'd always wondered about the value of journaling and writing in diaries, but maybe it did some good after all. I was holding in my hands the answers to many of the questions I had about my father. All I needed to do was read.

The words were neatly printed. I wish he had taught me to print so beautifully. I never had the patience for writing. I drifted through the first part of the book, taking in his love of nature. Trips to Tibet as a young man and his frequent visits with the Dali Lama. It seemed that he had been all over the world.

Then I came to the day of my birth. My heart burned as I read his words.

> *August 26, 1974*
> *Molay comes into the world.*
> *What a beautiful child.*
> *My heart is broken open.*

Underneath he had scribbled a short poem.

*My little girl awakens from the night to share her
light.
Oh world, you hold her tight and let her shine on
all.*

With tears streaming down my face, I turned the
page. A paper was clipped onto the page.

*March 16, 1976
The purple cross is the first line.*

I got shivers. He continued...

*This cross has been in my family since the time of
the Templars. It gives very strong powers to its
keeper. The keeper is chosen by the cross itself. I
was very blessed that it wanted me. It has already
chosen my Molay. Even as a baby she would take
it and smile. That is how I know. It would often
end up in her crib and I dare say how. I am
beginning to understand its power but Molay
will understand much more. She is a true Rose.
She will carry on my work to bring the hidden
into the light.*

I skipped to another entry dated November 11, 1977.

*I explained to Margaret that Molay was going to
do something special for the world. I had always
thought it would be me but it is her and I will help
her. She laughed at my absurd idea and said she
would do everything in her power to give Molay a
normal childhood. She forbade me to ever discuss
it with the child.*

Some normal childhood. Why would Mom not want
me to follow my path? Why she was so afraid?
Gratitude swept over me. She had discovered her light

and she was open now.

"Now is all there is."

Flipping through the pages, I landed on a poem by Rumi written in my father's elegant handwriting.

> *Love rests on no foundation.*
> *It is an endless ocean,*
> *with no beginning or end.*
> *Imagine,*
> *a suspended ocean,*
> *riding on a cushion of ancient secrets.*
> *All souls have drowned in it,*
> *and now dwell there.*
> *One drop of that ocean is hope,*
> *and the rest is fear.*

The poem that was on my dress the night I met Mr. Ahmadi!

"There are no accidents, my child."

I found a list dated May 16, 1978—visionaries he was studying. He wrote that the Mayans were not the only people to predict the end of the world. Incan and Egyptian calendars, as well as with the prophecies of Nostradamus, Edgar Cayce and Helena Blavatsky were mentioned in his notes.

I went to another paper-clipped page and read a formula that made no sense to me. Something about how to control the elements that he was obviously working on. He wrote that it came from Atlantean times, whatever that meant. Over the next few pages he'd written about the Hopi women. His descriptions about the Native American group's customs focused on weather control. The Hopi women held the secret and could manipulate the weather, but it was done with great respect.

> *If one is to attain such control, it must only be*
> *used for good. Control over the elements is*

achieved through sound and consciousness. Sound is first. I've been working with Molay on the sound vibrations since she started walking. We started with humming and will move to the more complicated tones soon. She picks up so quickly!

I could only remember us looking at the clouds a lot. Then I remembered the hum... oh my God!

January 3,1979
In the years after 2012, the feminine energy will be strong and we have a chance to bring out the hidden objects that we have hidden all over the world for safekeeping. They will make themselves known after 2012. They'll be brought together and a ceremony must be done.

On June 30, 1979 he had written a quote from a book *The Voice of the Silence* by Helena Blavatsky.

Help Nature and work on her; and Nature will regard thee as one of her creators and make obeisance. She will open wide her portals of her secret chambers.

He went on to give details of how he was experimenting with calming the ocean as he feared that the elements were angry with us humans. He felt the government was using weather control and it would backfire. There were certain astrological alignments in the coming years that could cause the ocean to rise and even bring tidal waves. He felt he could stop these earth changes from happening. He had discovered something powerful. There were lots of drawings and formulas that I could not understand. To the logical mind, his writings could have been judged as the work of a man losing his mind. But, the energy of the words felt so pure to me. I let my heart take the lead.

> *March 20, 1980 SPRING EQUINOX*
> *I want a new world for my beautiful Molay and all the other children of the world. I no longer trust much of what is told to me from others. I do not want to lose my innocence. Please God help me.*
>
> *I hear: Retreat and spend time in nature, or go looking for beautiful things to photograph, spend time with like-minded people, listen to inspiring music, create inspiring art.*
>
> *We can only help those who ask for it or are open to learning the truth and are asking for support as they do so. To try to force the truth on anyone is a waste of precious energy. We must save ourselves first. We must remain strong and rooted firmly to the earth. The new world is dependent upon us all staying strong. This is the moment we have long been training for.*
>
> *The secret is to breathe. All the Masters teach it. I will stay simple. I will breathe. I will follow the path of the Masters.*
>
> *Thank you God.*

He specified a date: November 6, 1980. On this date, he planned to surrender himself to the water and ask for peace. Self sacrifice? Is that what he was doing? No. I felt he was speaking directly to the great Mother in the ocean.

> *Oceana is the most powerful goddess.*

He also mentioned his brother Charlie who was

concerned and not interested in being part of any of it. Charlie wanted him to stop.

> *Charlie just doesn't understand it breaks my heart. One day he will understand.*

I guess my dad had very little support. I wish I had been old enough to help him. It must have been incredibly lonely. I fell asleep with the book in my arms.

Sally and I both got colds. We held court in my over-pillowed fortress of a queen size bed. I had a fever and her nose was running non-stop. Auntie told me we were cleansing from the dark night.

"Whatever," I barked.

The brown diary had not left my side.

"Sally, did Dad ever say anything about teaching me to change the weather?"

"Yes. I saw you do it with him twice, when you were just a toddler."

"Maybe this weather changing thing is just a coincidence," I said.

Shaking her head no she said we needed to continue to take the salt baths and drink lots of water. So that's what we did.

It took another week before we finally felt well enough to go outside. We sat in the courtyard of my building watching the clouds above us. I felt so grateful for those clouds, for the wind that moved them along, for the sun shining down on us. I was grateful to be part of it all, to be alive. I had passed through the dark night.

"I think it is time that you made an altar. You have been collecting all these holy objects so it is time to show some honoring. Appreciation. Gratitude."

"I feel a lot of gratitude, Auntie."

"I know you do, but actions speak louder than words, dear. Let's see. Why don't we use this table and move the television into the storage? You've got the one in the living room, you never watch this one. Remember that white doily I crocheted for you a few years ago?"

"Yes. It is in the top drawer of the buffet in the dining room."

"We will use that. Now we need a picture of the Mother, a glass of water, a coin, a candle and some incense."

I quickly gathered all that she wanted. This was the most energy I'd had in weeks. I felt genuinely excited. I presented Auntie with the statue that my mom had given me in Budapest.

"Quan Yin. Lovely. She is the Mother. Okay, now add the things that are meaningful to you. When you wake up in the morning you see them and give thanks. It helps to elevate your thoughts. Your thoughts create your life, Molly. Do you see?"

"Yes. I do. Look at what Mom gave me. It belonged to Grandma Vera. A relic of breast milk of the Virgin Mary. Where do you think she got this?"

"I know exactly where she got that. Sister Mary Margaret at the monastery gave it to her when she heard about your birth. Your mom was having a bit of trouble breast-feeding you and she thought it might help. Can you imagine what your mom must have thought? Well we will not go into that but your mom's milk did begin to flow. Your Grandma Vera treasured that beautiful piece. I am so happy you have it."

We fell asleep to a white candle burning on my new altar. The relics glimmered in the light. It was a night I will long remember.

That night I dreamt of the water.

I was on an island in the middle of the ocean. Mermaids came out of the water and took my hands. We all began to dance. I turned into a beautiful mermaid. Waking up abruptly, I ran my hands down my body to be certain that it wasn't real. Looking at

Dad's diary on the bedside table, I was now sure I'd been chosen for something special. I felt it with all of my being. I held the book close to my heart and prayed for guidance.

"You are not alone."

CHAPTER NINETEEN

I woke up on August twenty-sixth and the birthday texts, emails and cards starting rolling in. I love my birthday and have always insisted my friends make a big deal out of it. I've had birthdays that have lasted a month. This year was different. My traditional celebration felt a little ridiculous. I mean, what was the big deal about thirty-nine? I wanted to hide under the bed and just wait for next year when I would feel entitled to celebrate. My friends were trained, though. Even the ones I didn't speak to much these days did not forget my coaching.

Lisa officially started off my special day by delivering a soy latte and a croissant with a candle on it because I went to France so much. She also gave me a beautiful travel bag, all organized with little bottles labeled with everything I needed. Amazing. Who would have thought of that? My ex-boss sent over a case of cigarettes with a card. Did he really think I smoked those things?

Then the box arrived. Olivia knew how to make a girl feel loved! There was a fabulous silk scarf from Hermes called "Isis". The delicate material was decorated in blues and greens forming laurel leaves around a beautiful statue of a maiden. Next, a small red wallet for credit cards. Louis Vuitton. Very fancy. The last part of the gift was a jewelry box. Olivia loved jewelry and loved to gift it. When I opened it, *voila!* A golden mermaid with a pearl on her head and green emerald eyes sparkled at me. An exquisite little antique pin. Olivia became Oceana in that moment, joining with my father to affirm my new life.

I was admiring the little mermaid when my auntie came in with a bouquet of white roses from Karim Ahmadi. How sweet of him. The same roses as were everywhere in the room when we met. What a thoughtful man. I wanted a man who did things like that. Yes! I wanted a man who thought of me. I started making a mental list of what I wanted. Olivia told me to do it years ago. I wasn't quite ready back then. She suggested I write a list of one hundred qualities I wanted in a man. Then, I had to circle ten of them I couldn't live without.

I thought I would do the ten for now. After all, it was my birthday. I could do anything I wanted.

1. Thoughtful
2. Kind
3. Sexy
4. ESP- Available Emotionally, Spiritually and Physically (per Olivia)
5. Wants to get married
6. A gentleman
7. Independent
8. Loves to travel
9. Wants a family
10. Spiritual

Ten things. Done! Spiritual? I would have never thought of that one last year. Maybe I had already met him. Ankar?

"Let the flower open."

Olivia had arranged lunch at the Hotel Bel-Air and invited Penny Anne and Auntie. My precious little tribe. She was driving up but sent the gifts ahead so I could wear them. I dressed in a bit of a trance. I felt oddly peaceful with the mermaid on my dark blue dress as I moved my credit cards over to Louis Vuitton. Once I put the scarf around my neck, I changed my mind and decided to clip the mermaid to the scarf. Ah yes. It all worked perfectly. I wrapped my hair back in a bun at the nape of my neck and we were ready to go. As we were going down the elevator, another florist was coming up carrying a really unusual lavender lily. Of course it was for me, so we backtracked to my apartment and quickly left it inside on the table.

At the restaurant, we were seated at a table laden with gifts, candles and flowers. Surrounded by my adoring friends, I felt overwhelmed. I held back tears. Not the same kind of tears I'd experienced over the last few weeks that burned my chest and were so painful. These were tears were from being deeply touched. Vulnerable. Open. My shields had been melting. I was no longer the sensible, logical prove-it-to-me gal that I was last year. In the last nine months I had birthed myself. I felt extreme sensitivity to everything. The smells and voices in the room were almost too much for me.

Champagne started the meal compliments of Penny Anne. Of course, she insisted they add a touch of Chambord before we could toast. I held my glass up and acknowledged each one of them for what they brought into my life. Auntie, who had mothered me all my life and inspired me recently to accept and love myself. Olivia, who'd grown up with me and knew me so well… always nurturing me, listening to me, dressing me, and supporting me without fail. Penny Anne, my new friend, who had started my journey and changed my life.

"Cheers!"

Penny Anne blushed and put down her glass after toasting.

"Good Lordy, what in the world do you mean by that, honey?" she said, a bit too loudly.

The funny thing was I'd never talked to Penny Anne about the note in the cards. I just assumed she had seen it and read it and so I gave her a heads up when I found something new. Looking back at it all now, she must have thought I was nuts.

Olivia filled her in while I went to the ladies' room. When I returned Penny Anne insisted on seeing the note. I took it out of my purse and passed it around the table. As the conversation continued, I found out that Olivia actually bought my mermaid pin from Penny Anne, so they'd been talking "antiques" a lot over the last few weeks. Olivia pointed out the cross mentioned in the note and asked Penny Anne if she had seen such a thing. I hadn't mentioned the diary at this point because I wanted to ask Aunt Sally first. She nodded at me from across the table and smiled. She was reading my mind today.

Olivia had pre-ordered the meal and it just kept coming. Little bits of every taste possible. She said it was a year to open up the senses. She was right. Auntie was really enjoying the company, all dressed up in her, "let's sell real estate today!" suit and dark pumps. My favorite childhood birthday cake, red velvet, arrived along with olive oil ice cream. I felt like a queen. How could I go from such a dark place to feeling so happy? We humans are amazing creatures with the capacity for so many different emotions. I decided right then and there to explore them all. I wanted to feel life. I wanted to enjoy being alive.

Auntie held her glass up, toasting Olivia's engagement. She had still not given me the date. And not one word about the wedding over the last month. Maybe I had failed her as a friend by not showing enough interest? I just couldn't get excited about it and

I genuinely wanted to be happy for her.

"When is this beautiful day going to happen, Olivia?" Auntie asked.

"And might I add... what a beautiful rose our birthday gal will be as the maid of honor!" chirped Penny Anne.

Olivia went silent and her face paled. She quickly regained her composure.

"This is Molly's day! You'll receive your invitations as soon as we make all the decisions. Molly, would you like to open your gifts?"

Odd. And no interrupting calls from Kevin. The subject had been changed. Maybe I wasn't going to be her maid of honor? My heart sank. Auntie felt it and reached over our little table to present me with a small turquoise-wrapped box with seashells on it. I carefully opened it to find a ring with an insignia on it. My heart burned.

"It belonged to your father's family. His Masonic ring."

She had it sized to my finger. When I slipped it on it was a perfect fit. Electricity jolted my entire body. Jumping up, I ran around the table to her, hugging and kissing her till she begged me to stop.

"I love it, Sally! Thank you! Did it come from the box?"

"No. He gave it to Grandma Vera and when she died it came to me. I never wore it because I knew it was for you. I've been waiting to give it to you. It was something special to Hugh. He gave it to Mom after she admired it one Christmas. He had no money at the time and just slipped it off his hand and put it on her middle finger. He did things like that a lot. He called it spiritual yoga. Giving something away that you love deeply."

It reminded me of St. Anne and it must have struck a chord with Olivia because she looked into my eyes and nodded at me. I had an image of my father smiling at me. Proud of me. I dried my eyes as I sat back down. Receiving was never easy for me. Even though I loved celebrating my birthday, I didn't do it for the gifts. It came from being an only child, spending too many birthdays alone.

Penny Anne started giggling and handed me an envelope. It was a gift certificate to a psychic.

"What is this, Penny Anne? Do you go to someone?" I was shocked.

"Oh yes, at least once a year. I call it a tune up, darlin'… nothing I wouldn't do for my car. She's quite amazing and well worth the visit. She lives over there in the valley, you know? Just give her a call to set it up. And if you want me to go with you, I'll have my Jimmy run the shop. Okay, honey?"

"Okay." I felt nervous excitement. I had never been to a psychic before.

"Now, darlin'. For the love of all that's holy, do tell us where you are on this adventure of yours that I apparently started?"

Olivia took out St. Anne and put her on the table. She and I started giggling. I was wearing St. Therese and I pulled St. Joan out of my purse wrapped in a green suede bag. I hope Olivia didn't recognize the fabric. I cut up the suit she gave me so Sally could make protective bags for my finds. Dad's diary was also protected now, as well as the book. She'd made some extra ones for whatever else showed up. As I talked about everything that had happened, it felt good to share it all with this circle of dear friends.

I eventually talked about the diary and the purple cross. Auntie said she had not ever seen it or heard of it, but promised to look in the boxes that were in her barn. Olivia felt I should ask my mom about it. I agreed to ask, but I really didn't think she had it. She wasn't the type to hold on to old mementos. It had to be somewhere. Penny Anne suggested I find my uncle and ask him. That scared me. He had never reached out to me all these years.

"Ask the psychic about all this, sweetheart! You can ask her anything your heart desires. Make yourself a little list ahead of time, that's what I do."

That felt right. I would have to remember to do that.

The robe brought on a whole new level of conversation. Where did it come from? Where in the world did that gypsy come up with it? Was Pope Joan considered one of the saints? Auntie said anyone who had the courage to dress up and pretend like that deserved to be a saint. Penny Anne insisted it was because she had given birth while riding in a parade. I thought about the fact that none of us at the table had given birth. These were the most nurturing, supportive, loving women I had ever known. I guess all women find a way to mother.

"To love is to give all to all."

We were all holding hands as we waited for our cars. I kept thanking them and felt so happy to have this oddly compatible group as my tribe.

"Today, a flower has been born," Auntie said. "Your dad always told me that when women join together, something beautiful happens and a new flower is born. Women are the key to everything."

"Well, Lordy! I wonder what kind of flower we just made?"

Auntie and I smiled because we'd seen it before we left the house. The lavender lily.

"And might I add that whenever a flower is born, a bee is somewhere close by!" Penny Anne winked.

I came home to an orchid at my door with a beautiful note from Philippe, Marcus and Jose. The feminine power was recognized once again! My boys knew what I liked.

And who was the lavender lily from? I opened the card:

Happy birthday Molay. Wish I was with you.
Ankar

I carried the lily to my bedroom and placed it on my bedside table, right next to my dad's diary. I took my miraculous medal, kissed it, slid it inside the envelope with Ankar's card and tucked it under my pillow.

There were cards in my mailbox, e-cards in my inbox and a ton of texts. Just when I thought it could not get better, FedEx delivered a box from Madame. Inside was a small red drawstring bag monogrammed with the fleur-de-lis. It held an antique gold necklace with a bumblebee on it. Penny Anne was right, the bee just landed.

The day had been so beautiful except for the strangeness around Olivia's wedding. The fact that she hadn't mentioned the date or the role I'd play didn't sit right with me. Auntie sensed my tension and came over to rub my neck.

"Molly. I'm not so sure this wedding is going to happen. It doesn't have to do with you. Olivia isn't happy and she's in denial. This happens a lot. I have seen it so many times. The price is very high when you marry someone to support your mental dreams and not your heart dreams. She loves you very much, dearest. I want you to know that you are the light of my life, Molly. I'm sad to head back home tomorrow, but really glad I stayed for your party. Thank you for sharing this day with me."

She hugged me tightly and I was overcome with gratitude for this remarkable woman. At the same time my heart went out to Olivia, another remarkable woman. I didn't know she wasn't happy. How could I help her?

"Pray for her."

Just as I finished a prayer for Olivia my mother called. After singing happy birthday she couldn't hold back her excitement.

"Your new man Ankar just got the permit for the relic, he'll be sending it soon. He's quite wonderful,

Ankar. We've had him over twice for dinner and he impresses me more each time he visits. He talks about you all the time, Miss Molay. Forget about that dating service we talked about."

I was happy to hear that Mom and Bob had welcomed Ankar into their life.

"Do you remember that Molay was the name my father wanted to call me?"

"Hmmm. No. Maybe that's why I like it so much."

"The name Molay came from his relationship with the Templars. Right?"

"Oh, something like that. I don't remember, dear. It doesn't matter. It's a new day."

"Mom. It matters to me. Please let it matter to me."

"Yes, of course it does. I didn't mean to upset you. Oh, I'm really sorry. I just called to tell you about the relic and I messed it all up. I thought you'd be happy to know. I'm sorry, I was just trying to be helpful. I better let you go, dear."

"Mom?"

"Yes? Is something wrong? Have I done something wrong?"

"No. I was just wondering if you could tell me how to find my uncle?

"Yes. I can do that. Oh... where did I put it? I have his address here somewhere. It's pretty old, but it's something to start with. Here you go: 14789 Malibu Cove Road, Malibu, California, 90265. It's a small house right on the beach or at least it was. I have not spoken to Charlie for over 35 years. I heard he lived in Europe most of the time. Could you do something for me if you do find him?"

"Of course."

"Tell him 'hello' from me. Give him my love."

"If I see him I will. Thanks for the address."

"Happy birthday sweetheart. I love you."

"I love you too, Mama."

Hanging up the phone I wondered if I'd have the

courage to go to his door. I didn't expect to get his address just like that. I thought I'd have to do a little Nancy Drew sleuthing first. Looking at the address I thought, he knows I exist and yet I've never heard from him. Did he not like me for some reason? Would he reject me? It was too gloomy of a thought so I decided to wait. After all, it was my birthday and I could do what I wanted to… or was it cry if I wanted to? My mom used to play that song all the time.

CHAPTER TWENTY

The next week FedEx delivered another envelope. I opened my door to a camera flash. That same couple snapped a photo of me. They must have mistaken me for a celebrity. Silly people. Next time I would put on a hat and sunglasses and really mess with them.

Three days later I was boarding a plane to Istanbul, Turkey wearing my hot pink Juicy sweat suit. I had two deliveries to make. The first one in Istanbul with a couple of days to see the city, then on to Izmir to get the final signature.

This was a longer trip than I was used to. When I received the assignment, I was nervous at the thought of traveling alone to this part of the world. I'd heard terrible stories in the news about violence and their attitude towards women. I knew nothing about the Muslim faith or their customs and didn't want to offend anyone with my ignorance. The Internet was helpful for many of my questions, and I found out that Istanbul was ranked the "Happiest City in the World". Blake had arranged everything. I was totally taken care of and ready for an adventure.

After clearing Customs, I saw *Miss Molly Rose* written in tiny script on a sign held by a stocky dark skinned man. From the moment he picked me up he did not stop talking. His accent was so thick that I couldn't understand a word he was saying, so I just nodded my head in agreement every now and then.

He drove me to the hotel, in City Center right next to the Topkapi Palace. I felt the vivacious energy of Istanbul as I stepped out of the car. I marveled at the indigo, maroon and mustard colors on the beautiful domes of the mosques and palaces. It felt like a magical fairy tale. The hotel was perfect, with large white-washed balconies looking out over all those bright colors. Why was I here?

It felt almost sacrilegious to ask. My mind was doing its best to interfere, threatening to take me out of the experience. The whole city felt sacred, like a mosque or an altar. I decided to take a shower and refresh. Unpacking my bags, I placed the deck of cards on the bedside table. It had become a ritual to draw a card at the beginning of my adventures, so I shuffled them and picked one: *Beware of being deceived by others.*

Good to know. I would keep my eyes open.

After slipping into a summer pantsuit, I was off to explore. The front desk suggested I eat in the hotel before adventuring outside, but my stomach was not yet ready to ingest Turkey. My eyes wanted more of the rich colors. The marketplace was calling me. It was Tuesday and I'd read there was a massive market on the Asian side. It was a short forty-minute ferry ride away.

On the ferry, I struck up a conversation with Lucy, a young raven-haired American student. She looked like a model, but it turned out she'd been studying archaeology at Istanbul University for the last three years. Her older brother, Peter was also studying there. She invited me to join them for dinner the following night. Lucy was bright and fun and totally excited to show me the city. She said that Istanbul was hot and she wasn't talking about the weather! There were many happening places to go. In fact it was called the "World's Hippest City" too. Who knew?

Lucy and I walked around the market together chatting and laughing. Her language skills made my shopping spree a lot easier. She helped me buy gifts for everyone. I bought purple embroidered slippers for Olivia and me, golden silk bedspreads, beautiful tablecloths for Mom, Auntie and Penny Anne, and even a blue silk blouse to replace the one I tore up. Just as we were leaving the market, a little girl about six years old approached me. She wore a purple cross necklace. I remembered the line in the letter. It had to be a sign.

I followed her into a small alley to a tent-like structure. Lucy was apprehensive and tried to stop me but I insisted. I guess you didn't just do this sort of thing—following strangers into an alley. I felt no immediate danger. Something was calling me. We walked into the tent where her grandmother and several young men were quietly working on jewelry. The grandmother smiled a big toothless grin and handed me a tray of necklaces. One of the young men immediately ran around the corner and came back with copper cups full of coffee and some delicious flaky honeyed sweets. They were all so nice to us that I felt obligated to buy something. I kept looking for anything that could be part of the gift but it wasn't obvious until the child handed me a small metal case. Inside was a small sliver of wood mounted on some fabric.

"What is this?" I asked.

Lucy translated. The grandmother spoke rapidly in response. Lucy turned to me.

"She says it is a piece of table of the Virgin Mary."

It was not sealed and really looked like it had been made minutes before I arrived, but I bought it for one hundred Turkish lira because of the child.

As soon as we left the tent Lucy erupted like a volcano. "What were you thinking? You could have meals out for three days with that amount of money! You should've bargained with her. They expect that. You're being so stupid."

"It was about the child," I told her.

"She will never see that money. If you want to help her, why don't you go to Kiva.org and do a micro loan? The mothers in this country need a good education, put your resources there and it will ultimately help the child," she grumbled.

Putting the piece of table into my purse I shrugged. It wasn't her business how I spent my money. I really hit a nerve with that purchase. When we parted ways I could still see that my spending had irritated her, driving a wedge between us. I hoped that dinner was still on but said nothing.

That night I was serenaded by the exotic sounds of Turkish folk music pumping from the bar below. Turkey has this wild intoxicating energy and innovation that I had never experienced. The sexy, soulful music beckoned me into a deep sleep.

Loud knocking on my door forced me to wake up abruptly. I looked at the clock. Two thirty p.m. I had slept all day! My body clock was still on Los Angeles time. The maid wanted to come in and freshen my room. I jumped in the shower, dressed and went to the café downstairs for some of that famous Turkish coffee. There were only a few hours of daylight left, so I headed to see Stephan Church. Lucy had suggested it.

Wandering through the church I came across a medal much like the one I was given in Paris. A tiny silver miraculous medal was on the ground in front of an altar of Mary. I took it as a sign to sit down and pray. When I came out of prayer mode I could feel someone staring at me. There, across the aisle from me was the black man who had handed me my passport in Paris. The same man I'd seen with Marcus at the bar in the South of France. The hair on the back of my neck stood up. Running out of the church without thinking, I grabbed a taxi to the hotel.

Was it him? Could it have really been him? He seemed to recognize me but I couldn't be certain. When I arrived at the hotel, I discovered that I'd left the church without my purse. The driver didn't understand much English and was waiting to be paid. In a panic I ran into the hotel and asked someone at the front desk for help. They gave me some money to pay the driver and charged it to my room. I had to get back to the church. The only thing I could think of was to call my driver. Thankfully, I had left his business card in my hotel room. I called and asked him to drive me to the church to see if we could find my purse. He came right over and picked me up, but at the church my purse was nowhere in sight. He lectured me on safety all the way back to my hotel. In my head I went over the contents of my purse: two credit cards, about a hundred dollars in cash but luckily, no passport.

Back to the hotel, I went straight to my room to start calling my banks. As I dialed the first one there was a knock on my door. I opened it, expecting the driver with some news, but there on the navy blue carpet was my purse! I grabbed it, slammed the door and locked it. I stood frozen by the door, afraid to move a muscle, scared that the dark man was standing just outside waiting to grab me.

I'm not sure how long I stood there, but eventually I had to move. Checking inside my purse, I discovered the only thing missing was the piece of Mary's table. Funny, I hadn't felt the usual burning of my heart when I bought it. Maybe it was more important than I had thought. Changing my clothes so he would not recognize me, I put on a hat and sunglasses and hurried to the lobby. The front desk had no knowledge of my purse being returned. Whoever left it at my door knew exactly which room I was in.

I had about two hours to kill before dinner with Lucy and her brother, so I sat in the lobby bar incognito and had some bread with lots of olive oil and a cup of coffee. I was finally feeling a little calmer when someone touched me on the shoulder from behind. I jumped out of my skin! It was my driver just wanting to let me know he had left a message at the church and would continue looking for my missing purse.

"Oh my God, you nearly gave me a heart attack."

I pointed to my purse and told him the story. He shrugged and said something in Turkish to the bartender and we made arrangements for him to pick me up the next day at ten a.m. He would drive me to my meeting and then take me to the airport for my flight to Izmir.

I stayed in the bar, making friends with the staff until it was time for Lucy and her brother to pick me up, I waited tensely for a few minutes in the lobby. When they actually arrived I was flooded with relief. Still on after all. Lucy seemed happy to see me. She introduced me to her brother Peter, who was the male model version of her. An international law student, he looked to be in his mid thirties and was incredibly good-looking. He was so cute that I was thinking of creating a legal problem. But I could hear the voice of Olivia saying, "Never date a man who has the first name of a sexual organ." I couldn't stop smiling when I looked at Peter.

Lucy and Peter wanted to show me a Turkish nightclub to round out my Istanbul experience. They didn't feel the market or a church was fitting for my tourist visa. We went to Galata Tower, an amazing structure that seemed to stand sentry over İstanbul. Peter, playing tour guide, told me it was constructed in 1348. It was the tallest structure in the city for centuries, and still dominated the skyline. We went out to an upper balcony, which offered 360-degree views of the city. Spectacular!

Peter then took my hand and led me back inside the club to a table in front where Lucy had already taken her seat. Soon belly dancers were performing and pulling us out with them. I was so self-conscious. Luckily I managed to follow their lead and ended up having a great time learning how to swivel my hips. When we sat back down they asked us where we were from. One of them brought over a little American flag and put it in the center of our table.

Lucy excused herself around midnight. Peter and I continued to drink red wine and the entertainment went on until about two a.m. Neither one of us wanted to end the night but eventually we had to. He walked me to my hotel and kissed me tenderly on the mouth. As sweet as it was and as handsome as he was, it wasn't the kiss I had shared with Ankar in Budapest. I felt kind of guilty. On the elevator ride I texted Ankar that I really missed him.

The phone rang as I was getting ready for bed. Peter and Lucy wanted to accompany me to Izmir. They were full of ideas about what I should see and where we could go. There were some ancient sites they wanted to show me. They seemed so excited. I couldn't say no. I agreed and went to bed beaming. I love Lucy!

CHAPTER TWENTY-ONE

My driver was waiting downstairs for me at ten a.m. sharp. I had to stop him from taking my purse and locking it with my luggage in the trunk. Pointing to his eyes then at my purse, he gave me a very serious look. LOL. The delivery was fast and we were off to the airport.

Izmir is the third largest city in Turkey. I was scheduled to meet Mr. Dubois at the restaurant on the thirty-first floor of my hotel near Old Town. Arriving a bit early for the meeting, I took a table by a window with a gorgeous view of the bay. I was enjoying some homemade pasta when Mr. Dubois arrived. We did the kiss kiss and after thanking him for the birthday orchid we settled in like old friends.

"Well you made quite an impression on my brother, Miss Rose."

"He made quite an impression on me. Thank you so much for suggesting it. He was amazing and showed me such a great time."

"He sends his salutations with me today."

Mr. Dubois shifted uncomfortably in his seat and hesitated for a moment.

"With that said, I have a few things to discuss with

you. There seems to have been a breach in security over the last few months. Some inside information suggests that you are being followed. We were prevented from closing two important real estate transactions. Both involved your travel. It is essential that you keep very private about your dealings and meetings, especially your travel plans."

"Oh, Mr. Dubois. I have not told a soul what I'm doing. My family doesn't even know."

"Well, it may be someone who is in competition with Madame. She buys large land grants to save for future generations. There are many who want to develop these plots of land for financial gain, so there is some intrigue going on. Just be very careful and keep your eyes open."

I thought about the break-ins at my apartment and my hotel room in Paris, and then the loss of my purse in Istanbul. Now I felt nervous about Peter and Lucy who would be arriving tonight, staying here at the hotel. I really didn't know them at all. I couldn't afford to lose this job. I didn't say anything because how could I explain St. Anne speaking to me? Should I tell him about all the crazy things that seemed to be happening to me? I couldn't. Besides, it seemed so unconnected to these land purchases.

"We have some important exchanges coming up. Don't misunderstand me, Miss Rose. We are not unhappy with your performance. Quite the contrary, you have been very proficient. This may be something that is out of our hands. When you get into position there is often opposition. Just keep your eyes and ears open and continue to be discreet."

"Of course, Mr. Dubois."

He removed his glasses, cleaned them with his napkin and put them back on.

"Now, my brother tells me you have a bit of your own mystery going on. Perhaps I can be of service to you?"

"Really? What did he tell you?"

"He informs me that you are a collector of religious artifacts. Most unusual. I try to stay as far away from them as possible but I think it is because I was hit with too many rulers as a child in Catholic school. Did you experience this as well?"

"Oh. No. I didn't grow up with any religion."

"How divine! So rare to meet an innocent."

"Well, it didn't feel that way. When I had to fill out paperwork and write 'nothing' when it came to religion, it always felt so wrong. I wanted to belong to something."

"You are very lucky to not have all the dogma. Perhaps you can enjoy the purity of it all. The celebration of the saints is after all such a lovely idea. Our ancestors often mixed the bones of their deceased spiritual leaders with fluid and drank it. The bones are crystalline in structure so are thought to carry energy, power and transmit memory. With the holographic theory in mind, it seems that sitting with the bones or a hair of a saint would be just like sitting with the original person. Which ones do you want?"

"Open your heart. Tell him everything."

I told him about hearing St. Anne and then it all spilled out of me. I shared the whole story from Los Angeles to France to Budapest and showed him the note, which I always kept in my wallet. Then I took out the key. I told him I wasn't sure what it unlocked or what I was looking for. Finally, I admitted that I'd bought a piece of Mary's table and it had been stolen from my purse. It was such a relief to share it all with him. I literally felt lighter the more I spoke.

"So it was not a gift? You're telling me that you had money and credit cards in your wallet but the only thing missing was the little table relic? That's absurd, don't you think?"

I chuckled under my breath. So many odd things had been going on. I guess I was just getting used to it.

"I don't know what to think about all this. I've never had things like this happen to me before. I seem to be thrust into a whole new world. Now I'm wondering if someone is following me because of the mission that I'm on or because of the job I'm doing for you?"

"I can certainly understand the confusion. First and foremost, let's look at the note. Let me see here... oh, this is interesting. Seven sacred objects to be brought together with seven saints. Which ones do you have so far?"

"Well, I have a vestment of a pope—perhaps from the only female pope, Joan, an antique book on the life of the Virgin Mary, my father's Masonic ring and a key. But I don't know what the key is or if it means anything at all. I'm thinking that the table piece was just a mistake. I went to that stall because the child had on a purple cross and she seemed so insistent. The saints I've found are St. Anne, St. Therese, the Virgin Mary, St. Joan of Arc and St. Elizabeth. I'm missing two saints.

"I see. These objects may be quite separate from the seven saints. The purple cross is why you went to the stall—or 'manger'. The child is symbolic of you. Perhaps the purple cross is symbolic. I love such mysteries. As I said, there are very few innocents here. There are very few who have not been influenced by religion. You have a pure heart."

"I'm not so sure about that. I still don't know why I'm the one that St. Anne spoke to. She's with my best friend, Olivia now. She told me she wanted to be with her and I think I know why. Olivia has become so attached to the material world that it has taken her away from her own heart's desires. She's enmeshed in a relationship that she's not happy in, she's losing her sense of self. Maybe Anne is there to help her."

"I see, such a shame. Yes. But, is she an innocent?"

"No, I guess not. She went to Catholic school like you."

"Well then, let's stay on focus here. There are seven sins. The human body has seven chakras. Seven Wonders of the World. Why, there are even seven dwarfs! I believe these all represent an evolution of consciousness. We are in the midst of a consciousness revolution, Miss Rose. I am an Earth Watcher and I happen to be very tuned in to such things."

"What does that mean?"

This was getting stranger by the minute.

"I have the ability to see the chakras of the earth, the energy patterns of Mother Earth. There is a grid pattern that is affected by each one of us. Right now as we sit here we are interacting with our Mother. She is alive."

"I had no idea. How did you learn about all of this?"

"Well, I have certainly read everything that I have been guided to read, but most of my knowledge is something that I just seem to know. Of course, I've met a few others who feel the same way. One must trust oneself ultimately."

"Why not now?"

"I so agree," he said, responding to St. Anne.

"Did you hear her?"

"Hear what?"

"The voice that said, 'Why not now?'"

"Well I guess I thought you said that."

"I didn't say it. I promise you. It was St. Anne. You can hear her too!"

"Well then, it seems we are in this together."

He put his hand out and I wanted to kiss it. Instead I shook it and sealed the deal. I felt so grateful to have a comrade in arms.

"Mr. Dubois, do you think you might be able to help me?"

"Well, there are no coincidences. There are no chance encounters. I am sure that we've been brought together to further this work. My mission has been to serve Madame because I believe in what she's doing.

She has a great love for the earth and wants nothing more than to save this precious land for generations to come. I suppose in serving you I am still serving her. I do have a family friend who may have some insight into this shall we say 'unusual mission' that you are on. How long are you planning to stay in Turkey?"

"Three days. I'm not sure if I'm being followed or not."

"Let's assume you are for all intensive purposes. It's not wise for you to be alone here in Turkey."

"I have two friends from Istanbul that are flying in tonight. They plan to stay until I leave."

"I see. Very good. Do they know about your unusual mission?"

"No. They know nothing. Lucy was with me when I bought the table piece, but I didn't say much about it. I didn't have a chance. She got really upset with me for spending so much money on it."

"Please keep it that way. If you'd like, tomorrow after our transaction is complete I can take you all to Ephesus and we could perhaps have a few hours with my friend. I'm sure you'll find Ephesus very fascinating. It is the most well-preserved city of the Eastern Mediterranean."

I agreed thinking it was a great idea.

"Do you know about Sophia?" he asked.

"No, I don't."

"Well we are going to have an interesting time. Thank you, Miss Rose, for your time. Here's my card. Do not hesitate to call me should you need anything. I am staying at the hotel tonight in room 700 and will be at your service. Please be very careful. Do not open your door unless you know who it is. Promise me this."

I promised and left to prepare for my friends' arrival. I noticed a man watching me as I left the restaurant and took note of what he looked like. I had never seen him before. On the elevator ride to my room I realized I had a new sense of awareness about who was around me. Back in my room, I bolted my door and grabbed my cards. I shuffled and drew: *A mysterious gift will come your way*.

Just as I settled into the bath, my phone rang. It was Lucy saying they couldn't make it. Something had come up. She apologized profusely, saying she hoped we could see each other another time. I hung up the phone, a little disappointed.

"Everything is perfect."

I fell asleep to a rerun of *Dancing with the Stars*. It must be a big hit in Turkey.

First thing in the morning, I called Mr. Dubois to tell him that I was on my own. He didn't seem surprised. He suggested that we check out of the hotel. He felt it wasn't safe and had found another one near Ephesus with two rooms available. Fine by me. We agreed to meet in the lobby in thirty minutes. I packed my bag and wheeled it down to the lobby to meet him.

When our meeting time came and went, I got a little nervous. I kept trying to call Mr. Dubois but got no answer. An hour passed. Now I was concerned. Out of the corner of my eye I saw a beautiful woman standing next to me. As had happened before, when I turned to face her she was not there. I could feel her power though, like a shield. A tall man, somewhat familiar but I couldn't put my finger on it approached me. He informed me that Mr. Dubois had asked him to drive me to the airport. Why would Mr. Dubois have not told me this? We were not planning on going to an airport.

"Where is Mr. Dubois?" I asked.

"He's been detained in a business meeting."

The man was sharp with me. My stomach began to hurt. Something was not right. I pressed further with questions and he grew tense, motioning to another man who came towards me.

"Why don't we just get in the car and we'll talk

about all of this?" the first one said.

Use honey, I remembered.

"Ok, perfect!" I feigned, "Mr. Dubois is so thoughtful to have you two gentlemen escort me. Oh dear, I forgot something in the room. I'll be right back. Can you watch my suitcase please? My passport and all my important work papers are inside." I lied, holding my room key up high.

I hope I didn't use a Southern accent when I said all that because I sure felt like Penny Anne just then. They seemed caught off guard, but agreed to wait for me.

I couldn't get to my room fast enough. First thing, I called the front desk and spoke with the manager who had checked me in. Thank goodness he remembered me and would help. I quickly explained that I was concerned about Mr. Dubois and asked him to meet me at room 700. In a flash we were there together knocking on the door. There was no answer but we could hear a muffled sound coming from inside the room. Someone was struggling. The manager quickly opened the door and the sight that greeted us stopped my heart.

The room was torn apart at the seams. Mr. Dubois was tied up to the bed, bound and gagged. He looked so relieved to see us. The manager immediately dialed the police while I untied Mr. Dubois. After calling the police, he told the front desk to keep an eye on the two men until the police arrived. Thank God I had listened to myself.

"I'm sorry, Miss Rose. I am so relieved that you are safe. When they knocked on my door I called out your name thinking of course it was you."

Poor Mr. Dubois. When the phone rang we all jumped. It was the front desk saying the police were on their way up to the room, but the two men had gone. They left in a black Mercedes with darkened windows just before the police pulled up. The doorman remembered diplomatic plates being on the car when he tried to help them put a suitcase into the trunk. Luckily, all my important things were actually in my purse, including my passport.

Six heavily armed military police officers entered the room. I was clearly not in the United States now. One stayed at the door while the others marched in, searching the room with precision. The officer in charge asked us to describe the men. As Mr. Dubois was describing them, it hit me. The taller of the two men, the one who seemed familiar—I had seen him before.

"I've seen one of them before. He and some woman have been outside my apartment snapping photos of me off and on for months now."

Mr. Dubois looked shaken.

"I thought they were tourists and had mistaken me for a celebrity. It didn't dawn on me that I was being followed."

Once the police had gathered all the information they needed, they told us we could go. They said they would be in touch if they had any questions or found the suspects. Mr. Dubois quickly made a phone call and after a few minutes of conversation hung up shaking his head. For the moment, there would be no transaction. Another plan was in motion. We were instructed to shred all paperwork immediately.

As we shredded the paperwork in the manager's office Mr. Dubois chuckled to himself.

Curious, I asked, "Does this mean Madame lost the land?"

"Oh no, Miss Rose. It will happen. It just means we will not be involved. She will find out who is behind all of this. Maybe even before the military police do!"

Mr. Dubois called his driver and in no time we were in the car headed out of town.

CHAPTER TWENTY-TWO

The further we got from Izmir the better we both felt. We were on the road for about an hour with very little conversation. Lost in my thoughts about what had just happened at the hotel, I knew I had to stop trying to figure it out. My stomach felt a little queasy so I cracked the window for some fresh air as we made our way into the lush green mountains. Turning off the main road, we were greeted by a magnificent statue of the Mother. My heart burned. I had to take a moment to catch my breath.

"Meryemana," the driver remarked.

"What did he say?" I asked Mr. Dubois.

"This is Meryemana, the house of the Virgin. It is the last known residence of the Virgin Mary, mother of Jesus Christ. It is a very special place for both Christians and Muslims. She spent the last part of her life here. I thought you'd enjoy having a quick tour before we go meet my friend."

The driver pulled into the small parking lot to drop us off. Mr. Dubois told him to stay close as we wouldn't be long. The grounds were gorgeous. Set on a hill, there were beautiful gardens with a few benches here and there. The house itself was a small structure made of stone nestled under the forest canopy. There were tourists outside the main door, reading the plaques that described the history of the house. A few people were milling about taking photos and there were others standing in front of a stone wall covered with what looked like crinkled pieces of paper. Mr. Dubois explained that it was called a "wishing wall". People wrote their intentions on paper or fabric and tied them to the wall.

The whole place had a sacred vibration. I felt it as soon as we drove on the property and it got stronger the closer we got to the house. We were greeted warmly at the chapel door by a young woman who seemed to recognize Mr. Dubois. She ushered us inside and introduced us to Sister Nihel who received us with a smile, greeting Mr. Dubois in French. The young woman bowed and left. Sister Nihel was one of two resident nuns who recited prayers in the chapel daily. A tiny woman with large dark doe-like eyes, she looked elfin. The entire universe sparkled in her eyes. I thought I saw smoke around her. Was she real? I really had to wonder.

She welcomed us both and in a hushed tone began telling us about Meryemana. As she spoke, she kept looking at my chest. She knew about the St. Therese under my blouse!

Sister Nihel explained that we were in the chapel. There were other people in the small stone room, kneeling, praying on an ornate rug that had been spread across the stone floor. Their focus of attention was a large altar covered with flickering white candles. White roses in simple vases flanked a gold cross standing regally in the center. Behind the altar stood a large statue of the Virgin Mary. I wish I could properly describe how I felt in that room. It was the most benevolent presence I'd ever experienced. Pure love. Pure peace. The sister motioned for us to move along, she had more to show us. I followed her reluctantly.

She walked us to Mary's bedroom on the right side of the house. It was simple and austere. Not much there. One tiny window offered up a small ray of sunlight. I noticed a small hole in the floor that the sister explained led to a spring that ran under the house. But again, the presence was intense.

Sister Nihel turned to me and asked, "Sister Joan may I offer you something to drink?"

My jaw dropped. She didn't wait for my answer and walked away with a mysterious smile on her face. Mr. Dubois didn't seem to notice that she had called me by the wrong name. She reappeared moments later with a glass of water. Gliding across the room, she handed it to me. I could swear her feet never touched the floor.

That was it. Those were the only rooms to see. As we left the bedroom and walked outside, Sister Nihel told us more about the spring. It was believed to have healing properties. She led us over to a wide circular hole in the ground where the spring flowed up, a shallow looking well. There were tourists gathered around it, touching the water with the tips of their fingers then making the sign of the cross over themselves. A few of them were seated beside it, praying. I got a strange feeling that we were near the end of the tour.

"Would you mind if I take a few minutes in the chapel before we leave?"

"Go right ahead, Miss Rose," Mr. Dubois said, nodding. "We'll be here when you are ready to go."

I entered the chapel. I hadn't noticed it before, but there was a stream of sunlight coming down from the ceiling. Alone in the small room, I shifted into some sort of autopilot mode. It felt like an altered state. My body moved of its own accord. My legs guided me along, right in front of left until I was standing directly in front of the altar. My gaze went down below the altar to a cabinet door with a small keyhole. I was instantly drawn to the keyhole. It didn't actually speak to me in words, but it called me loud and clear. My heart was afire. The beautiful woman appeared in front of me and walked around to stand behind me. She was shielding me from sight. I could feel it!

"You have the key."

My hand reached into my purse, took out the key and put it into the keyhole. It fit perfectly. I felt what seemed like an electrical current run from the keyhole through the key and down through my body into the earth. The tips of my fingers and toes tingled. With a little muscle the lock clicked open, creaking. I closed my eyes for a moment, feeling like a museum thief.

"Your destiny is inside. Be not afraid."

I could tell the door had not been opened for a very long time. Slowly, carefully while holding my breath, I coaxed it open. Sweat dripped from my forehead. Just inside was a small bundle that my hand blindly removed and tucked into my purse. Something wrapped in swaddling cloth. My hand, still on autopilot, closed the cabinet door, locked it and slipped the key into my pocket. I fell to my knees and assumed the prayer position, praying to the Virgin Mary for her guidance. My heart was praying. My body was praying. I prayed with every fiber of my being. My body did it with willingness and with obedience.

Some benevolent force raised me up and as I turned to leave, I saw I was not alone. There were at least a dozen tourists sitting facing the altar! They didn't appear to see me, even as I made my way out of the room. When I crossed the threshold and the sun hit my face, I was immediately back in my body again, back in the driver's seat. It felt like a dream. Reaching into my purse, I touched the cloth to be sure it was real. I must have appeared a little shaken as I joined Mr. Dubois and Sister Nihel because he asked if I was okay.

"Yes, fine. Thank you. I just wanted to spend some time in the chapel. This is such a special place."

They both agreed. Mr. Dubois announced it was

time for us to go and Sister Nihel handed me a small amber glass vial with clear liquid inside.

"Water from the spring to take with you on your journey. Thank you for visiting us today. The Mother is so grateful to you for your service."

I accepted it and hugged her. Something shifted inside of me. I could hear her thoughts. She knew everything! Tears burned in my eyes. Part of me wanted to pull the object from my purse and give it to her, but I knew it was my destiny.

Just then, she pulled away and bowed slightly with her hands in prayer.

"Go now in peace. You are never alone. God bless you, sweet child. The Mother gives her gifts to those who are willing."

"Yes, you are loved."

CHAPTER TWENTY-THREE

Mr. Dubois and I said very little on the way to Ephesus. I didn't breathe a word about what had just happened in the chapel. As we approached the city, he instructed the driver to drop us off at the library. A short stocky man was standing in front waving to us as we pulled up.

"There is 'The Cak'! He is a legend around here. Believe me, Miss Rose, we are very fortunate to have been given this audience with him on such short notice. If you needed a sign, this is it."

We stepped out of the car and found ourselves face to face with the master.

"Miss Rose, allow me to introduce you to Mr. Ersin Cakmak. Ersin, this is Miss Molly Rose."

"Just go ahead and call me Cak Miss Rose, everyone else does," he said, chuckling as he extended his hand and made a small bow. His full head of gray hair and bushy beard hid his eighty-five years well. The two men exchanged pleasantries briefly in French.

"Cak has been with the library for over sixty years. He is the world expert on ancient texts and languages. You can safely share your story with him, Miss Rose. I think he may be able to help you along."

The three of us made our way through the library to Cak's office. As soon as the door was closed, I began to recount the extraordinary course of events from the beginning. Cak listened intently to my story and at one point I showed him the letter. As he read it his eyes lit up with recognition. He asked me to list the items I had found so far. I named the items one by one as I'd done with Mr. Dubois earlier. Going to a shelf at the back of his office, he pulled out a thick leather bound book.

"Miss Rose, you are part of an ancient plan that I have long heard about. It involves seven women who were known as the Seven Sisters. The Seven Sisters originated as far as we know in Greek Mythology. They were the seven daughters of Atlas and Pleione. Ultimately, they had a star cluster named after them called the Pleiades. Have you heard of the Pleiades?"

"Yes. It's a constellation. Right?"

"Correct. So, the Pleiades are the Seven Sisters. Do you follow?"

"Yes, I think so."

"Good. The Pleiades star cluster is located at one of the nodes, or points of intersection between the galactic and super galactic planes. Nodes represent star gates, which are inter-dimensional portals and pathways for accessing higher-dimensional realities. The ancient Greeks, Egyptians, and Maya oriented their temples and pyramids towards the Pleiades. The Parthenon, the Great Pyramid at Giza and Teotihuacán near Mexico City are also structures built in alignment with the Pleiades. And there are many, many more. In India, the Pleiades have been referred to as the Seven Mothers of the World. There are also several Native American creation stories in which they identify the Pleiades as their ancestors who came to this world as Starseeds, or bringers of light and knowledge."

He pointed to illustrations in the book as he spoke in excited bursts, his overgrown eyebrows bouncing up and down.

"Now, there are seven holy objects on the earth that have been hidden from the masses to be brought out when the time was right. Based on the note you have, I guess it is time for them to appear. I believe the woman who wrote this note was the great Madame Blavatsky, cofounder of the Theosophical Society. If my memory serves me right, she died in London a year after this note was written. Madame Helena Blavatsky was the fountainhead of modern occult thought."

"Oh my God, my dad wrote about her in his diary!"

"That doesn't surprise me, you must have quite the bloodline. As far as the purple cross, I've heard about its existence. It supposedly contains relics from the Crucifixion of Christ. It last belonged to Pope John VIII or Pope Joan depending on what you believe. It was thought to have been buried with the corpse and perhaps grave robbers took it and put it back into circulation. I have not heard it mentioned since I was a young man. It is believed to have magical powers."

He pulled out another book and showed me a rendering of the purple cross. It was larger than I had imagined.

"Cak, I recently read in my late father's diary about the purple cross. It has been in my family for many generations, but I have not been able to locate it. I had no idea what to look for. Oh, and then there's this." I carefully unwrapped the bundle I had in my purse.

Inside the bundle was an iridescent stone carved like a tortoise shell. It was glowing and there was something carved on it. Perhaps words? A note was wrapped around it. Handwritten in German, it was signed Catherine Emmerich.

Cak looked at the note and his eyes almost popped out of his head.

"It is the Oracle... holy Mother of God! You have in your hands the Oracle of Delphi!" he howled.

Mr. Dubois was visibly stunned. "Well where in the world did that come from?" he asked.

Pulling the key out of my pocket, I said, "At Meryemana, when I went back inside the chapel. Under the altar there was a little door with a lock on it. St. Anne told me to use the key. The key fit and when I turned it the door opened. The bundle was inside and I took it with me. I was guided. It didn't even feel like I was in charge of my body when the whole thing happened. When I left I saw there were people in the room. None of them could see me, it was like they were looking through me at the altar."

"Of course you were not in charge, dear woman. This is the Oracle of Delphi we are talking about!" Cak reassured me.

"But I thought the Oracle was a shrine in Greece?" I was completely confused.

"The shrine was built for it, but the Oracle itself was never found. It was rumored to have been taken by one of the maiden priestesses. This note is from Sister Catherine Emmerich. She was a German mystic who had more visions and premonitions than all the other saints combined. We owe the finding of Mary's house to her. As the story goes, Sister Emmerich was an invalid confined to her bed with signs of the stigmata on different parts of her body. Over the years—"

"Wait, can I ask you something? What is the stigmata?" I asked.

"Oh, I'm very sorry. I just assumed with all of this... are you not Catholic Miss Rose?"

"No, I'm not. I was not raised with any religion."

"Oh my," he said, smiling. "An innocent. I had no idea," he said with a chuckle as he pulled out another book to show me a photo.

I noticed Mr. Dubois had a large grin on his face.

"Yes. Well, stigmata is a name for wounds or markings in the areas matching the crucifixion wounds of Jesus Christ. Officially documented by the Roman Catholic faith, many reported stigmatics were members of religious Catholic orders, such as nuns or monks. Do you understand?"

I nodded. It sounded gruesome.

"Good. So, Sister Emmerich was not well. In 1812 at the age of thirty-eight, she was confined to her bed and someone taking care of her observed the stigmata. The open wounds continued to manifest on her body for years. It must have been tremendously painful. Can you imagine? During this time, she had many visions. In one, she chronicled the journey of the Virgin Mary and Apostle John from Jerusalem to Ephesus after Jesus' resurrection. On a mountain in Ephesus, John built a stone house for Mary where she lived out the rest of her life. Sister Emmerich described Mary's house in vivid detail. It was all recorded at her bedside by a famous poet named Brentano. Years after the visions, a Frenchman read Brentano's account and set out for Ephesus to find the house. The structure at Meryemana is what he found. It was exactly as Sister Emmerich had described."

"Do you think that the oracle was the reason she had the visions? And these words," I said, pointing towards the note. "What does she say here?"

"It is most likely the oracle that created these accurate visions. The words are 'know thyself'. Did you notice the blood on the paper of both notes?"

"Yes."

"Both of them connected their lives to this mission. Sealing something with one's own blood is a very ancient and sacred ritual. This note is a relic, child. This is one of the seven saints you are looking for. Can you imagine a women who is an invalid doing this? Brentano must have helped her."

"What do I do with this oracle?"

"The note indicates it will be found by the person who is to use it for prophecy. I cannot direct you Miss Rose. I'm afraid I'm only an expert on language and the past. The future is yours to create."

"Thank you, Cak. If I can not do it, what happens?"

"I realize that it is a big responsibility but believe me when I say that if you found it—you have what it takes. But of course if you say 'no' to the universe, someone else will arrive. It is essential to the well being of our world that this be done. Good luck to you. Now I must go for my midday nap. It has been my great pleasure, Miss Rose."

I rewrapped the oracle and put it in my purse, said goodbye and we left.

Heading down the library steps, Mr. Dubois walked beside me like a priest. As we slowly descended the stairs, I had a déjà vu. Yes, I had definitely done this before. Somewhere. Sometime.

"Time does not exist."

At the bottom of the library stairs, I came face to face with Sophia. Four statues along the outer wall set in recesses contained female statues representing wisdom (Sophia), knowledge (Episteme), intelligence (Ennoia) and virtue (Arete). Interesting that these virtues were represented by women.

"Why did you ask me if I knew about Sophia?"

"It seemed important at the time. Now I understand why. In order to have the oracle, you must employ wisdom regarding when and how to use it. Please know that you will always have all the help you need."

Our driver was patiently waiting for us in front of the library. Mr. Dubois directed him to take us to Selcuk.

"I've arranged rooms for us at a lovely hotel Miss Rose. It has been quite an adventure today. It will be a good place to relax before we fly home tomorrow."

I felt so grateful for his thoughtfulness. I really needed to go somewhere quiet and calm to process everything.

While Mr. Dubois was checking us in, I shopped in the gift store. There was a beautiful swimsuit I just had to have, some clothes and a few toiletries to replace what I lost in my suitcase. Mr. Dubois kindly told me to charge everything to his room- a business expense. As soon as I got to my room, I pulled a card: *You receive help and assistance to solve a problem.* There was a framed quote on the wall above the bed:

> *Grant me the serenity to accept the things I cannot change, the courage to change the things I can, and the wisdom to know the difference.*
>
> Saint Francis of Assisi

"Please, St. Francis guide me to know the difference," I prayed.

I was in a situation that I could not change. It had happened. I now had in my possession an ancient stone. Possibly a meteorite. Mr. Dubois thought it could be a stone-iron meteorite which apparently was very rare.

"There is much mythology associated with the Pleiades star cluster, Miss Rose," he mused at dinner.

I could remember gazing at it as a child. It was one of my favorites. The Pleiades is such a conspicuous object in the night sky.

"Are you kidding? I spent my childhood looking at it."

A vague memory of sitting with my father outside at night ran through my mind. He was teaching me about stars. He was explaining the universe. I couldn't hold on to it. The vision passed so quickly. I wanted it back.

"Miss Rose, is everything alright? You look tense, and you haven't eaten anything on your plate."

"Yes. Just memories passing through. So much to take in, I'm a little overwhelmed and a bit anxious. I can't eat anything right now. Mr. Dubois, do you think you could call me Molly?"

"If you like, Molly. Please call me, Philippe."

"That seems weird. For some reason I can't do that,"

I laughed.

"Then let's just keep things as they are. Shall we?"

"Yes, let's do that."

It felt good to laugh.

"And now I think we should say goodnight, Miss Rose. You look very tired. A good night's sleep is in your very near future."

"Thank you for everything. You have been so kind and thoughtful at every turn. I could not have done any of this without you."

Kiss kiss and I was off to my room. As soon as my head hit the pillow I was out for hours. This adventure had been exhausting plus I felt like I was getting a cold.

I woke up at two a.m. staring at the little bundle on the nightstand. It was glowing through the cloth, or was it my imagination? I lay there staring at it for a long time and could not coax myself back to sleep. I needed to move, to walk. Something. I felt terribly anxious. I had to get out of the room.

The hotel had a pool, so I put on my new swimsuit and a pair of jeans and slipped quietly outside. Thinking of my dad, I wished I had learned to swim. I dipped into the shallow end and got wet, then moved into the warm spa and reclined, gazing at the sky. The Pleiades twinkled at me. There was no moon, only a vast sky dotted with thousands and thousands of beautiful stars. I was immersed in stillness, in peace. When the water got too hot for me, I curled up on a lounge chair to cool off. The breeze danced over my body, rustling the leaves of the trees standing watch over the pool area. All my senses were heightened. I felt alive. I could feel life all around me and I knew I was part of everything and everything was part of me. No separation.

I went back and forth between the spa and the lounge chair a few times. I knew hours passed because the sun was on the horizon when I got out of the water for the last time. I toweled off and put my jeans on over my wet swimsuit. In my pocket I felt the holy water, hard glass against my soft skin. It gave me a safe feeling, like I had a lucky charm. I glanced at the clock as I left the pool. It was six a.m.

I felt completely peaceful as I made my way back to my room. As I put my key card into the lock, a large man grabbed me from behind and another one put a gag in my mouth, taping it shut. Then, something was put over my head and I couldn't see anything. I tried to scream, but the tape muffled my voice. One of them grabbed my legs and they carried me away kicking and screaming.

My hands and feet were bound and I was put into the back seat of a car. Feeling afraid for my life and so disoriented, I had no idea which direction we were driving. Even when they removed the covering from my face and I could see, I still couldn't figure out where we were. But I did recognize the men, the same two men from the hotel in Izmir. After about an hour they stopped at an oven bread stand and bought several loaves. One of the men removed the tape from my mouth and handed me a warm loaf of bread. The smell is something I can still bring to my senses. The first bite was intoxicating. I was famished and gobbled up the entire loaf. To this day I swear it is the best bread I have ever eaten in my entire life.

I have always felt car sick on winding roads and I tried to tell them. After asking them to open a window to no avail, I laid my head down on the leather seat and closed my eyes. Time passed. They talked what they would do next, getting more and more excited about how much money they could get for my return. I prayed to all my saints and to my father to please help me. Suddenly, I felt dizzy and sick to my stomach. Gagging, I vomited on the floor of the car. Both men seemed genuinely caught off guard. I begged them to stop at a bathroom so I could clean myself up. They argued in Turkish till we came to a stop in a small town. There were quite a few people around, and the pair looked a little nervous. The driver reached under the seat and pulled out two guns, which they each tucked inside their jackets. He walked around to the back seat and roughly removed the binding from my hands and feet. After warning me to keep my mouth shut, he motioned towards a busy café. They followed closely behind me.

The ladies room had two stalls. I took my time, hoping someone else would come in. Sprinkling the holy water over my body I said a prayer and took a deep breath. The door opened and a woman about my size walked in. Thankfully she spoke English. Begging her for help, I told her about the two men and asked her if she would be willing to change clothes with me. She agreed. Her husband was the owner of the café so she assured me she would be safe. I put on her clothes, wrapped her scarf around my head and calmly walked out, right past the two men!

The next thing I knew I found a ride with a retired couple from Ohio on their way to Ephesus. They were staying at my hotel and they'd be happy to give me a ride. Back at the hotel, I ran to my room and called Mr. Dubois.

"We have to leave right away! We have to get out of here!" I was shaking.

I told him what had happened and that the men surely would be on their way back to find me. It was not safe to stay at the hotel another minute. I grabbed my things and met him at his room.

We both agreed that shredding the papers had been a wise move, Madame would be pleased with us. He called the driver and we were in a car within twenty minutes, heading back to Istanbul. I mentioned the holy water and what happened when I used it.

"Do you have any of the water left?" he asked me.

LAURA BUSHNELL

"No. I used it all. Should we go back and get some more?"

"Yes. Most definitely."

The driver did a U-turn and within fifteen minutes we were back in the gift shop of the House of Mary. We each bought a dozen bottles.

"Miss Rose, something we are about to do must be very controversial."

"You think so?" I said, laughing. "Imagine that!"

On the drive to the airport Mr. Dubois called the military police officer who had given us his card. They would meet us at the International Terminal. The next phone call was to Blake as we were in need of new flight arrangements. When we finally got to the airport the police told us that the two men had been apprehended. We were shown photos of the suspects, quickly identified them and were free to leave. Thank God they were found. Mr. Dubois made sure I was safely on board my flight before he took his flight back to Paris. Why in the world was this happening to me?

"You accepted the gift."

CHAPTER TWENTY-FOUR

After a couple of painfully long layovers and a nasty rainstorm, I wanted to kiss the ground when I finally arrived in Los Angeles two days later. I was looking over my shoulder the entire trip, my anxiety was through the roof and I think I made it home on pure adrenaline. Needless to say, I was exhausted. New treasures in tow, I couldn't get home fast enough. I turned off my cell phone and took to my bed, sleeping for twenty-four hours straight.

When I finally woke up there was a message from Blake on my voicemail. Mr. Dubois had concerns about my safety at home. Even though the two men had been apprehended, they were part of a much larger organization. The company had hired a private security guard to watch my apartment. Blake promised he would be very discreet and his sole purpose was my safety. Thank God, no more fake paparazzi!

The next day I did some research. Pulling the note out of my purse, I laid it on the desk beside my computer. I'd memorized the words by now, but I read them again for the zillionth time:

To the occult student who has found
this note:
I beg of you to help me. I was given
a vision as a young girl to find seven
sacred objects and bring them together
with seven women. Henry feels this is
crucial for the changes the earth is
making. We are moving into a new age.
An age of peace and enlightenment —
the return of the feminine. You will be
guided every step of the way but it
will require a sacrifice at times. If
each step were not so reinforced it
would be impossible. I started the
journey and I leave its completion to
you. You have been chosen. There are
seven saints for seven sins.

Фиолетовый крест правит вечно.
Запланировано было всё, время и
место. Вы - Роза.

Helena 1890 London.

I did a Google search on Madame Helena B. Her full name popped up before I could finish. Helena Petrovna Blavatsky was a Russian-German occultist born in 1831. During her lifetime, she'd traveled the world learning about ancient wisdom and religion. In 1875, Madame Blavatsky and her partner Henry Alcott established a research and publishing institute known as the Theosophical Society.

I looked at the note again and read:

*Henry feels this is crucial for the changes the
earth is making.*

Shivers. I was riveted as I continued to read the bio.

The Theosophical Society officially launched a
movement that caused Madame Blavatsky to be quite
controversial. She went on to publish an extensive
amount of work on spiritualism—all written in
English. Criticism over her writing and ideas
continued even after her death in 1891. Looking back at
the date on the note, any question I'd had about her
being its author dissolved.

The word occult scared me and fascinated me at the
same time. When I thought of it, I thought of Satan
worshippers or weird rituals with sacrifices. I did a
Google search to discover it was officially defined as
knowledge of the hidden. Knowledge of the hidden?
Based on that definition, I was now a student of the
occult. My father definitely was and likely my
grandmother Vera. Aunt Sally too! It seemed occultists
crossed all the gender, cultural, religious and age
barriers. There was nothing spooky or scary about it at
all.

Okay. So, Madame B's note had mysteriously come
into my hands. Since then, I had been directly guided
to these sacred objects while learning about the seven
sins. I looked at the translation of the Russian in the
note I'd written down at lunch so long ago:

*The purple cross forever reigns. The time and
place have all been planned. You are a Rose.*

I knew from Dad's journal that the purple cross had
been in my family for generations. The obvious next
step was finding it. I sensed my father smiling at me
now, beaming with pride, happy I was finally putting

this all together.

But wait a minute. What about the seven women?

"All will be revealed. The purple cross forever reigns."

Over the next couple of days I got myself unpacked and back to my routine. Early on the morning of the fourth day Lisa called to see if I wanted to do an impromptu hike in Runyan Canyon. I needed the fresh air and exercise, so I told her I'd pick her up on the way and headed out the door. I saw the security guard sitting in his car in the parking lot. We hadn't been formally introduced but I knew it was him.

Lisa didn't say much at the beginning of the hike but something was obviously wrong. In the middle of talking about nothing, she finally opened up. Her husband wanted a divorce. No wonder she wanted to see me. When she finally started telling the story she hardly took a breath, unburdening herself for the first time. She hadn't told anyone. Listening to her I felt compassion like any good friend would, but I experienced an odd sense of disconnect.

"Oh, Molly, I'm a basket case! What do you think I should do?" she asked me.

"You don't have to do anything. When you get home today, he'll call you and tell you that his mother has been diagnosed with cancer. He'll say he's sorry he has been so distant and he doesn't want to end the marriage. That's it. You'll have a baby next year."

I don't know where my response came from. It just flowed right out of me in a very matter-of-fact way. From the look on her face, she was horrified.

"What? Where the hell did that come from? Are you making fun of me? Why would you say something like that? I was so stupid to share any of this with you."

She stomped down the hill and left me standing there.

I didn't mean to offend her. Why did I say those things? Crazy. I felt bad that I had said anything. As I headed back to the trailhead, I began to hear the thoughts of people walking by me. A woman thought: *I think I am late, I need to pick up some milk.* Another man thought: *Nice legs.*

"Thank you," I said, smiling at him.

He stopped, looked me in the eye and thought: *Did you read my mind?*

"Maybe," I winked.

He laughed and walked off. I felt like I was in a movie, or some sort of altered reality. It frightened me and was oddly fun at the same time. When I got back to the trailhead, no Lisa. I texted her an apology and told her I was heading home just in case she needed a ride. No response. When I got in my car I there were seven sisters in full habit sitting there with me.

I was losing my mind.

Definitely time for a shrink. I called Mac and left a message saying I needed to talk to his sister's doctor as soon as possible.

Just as I got home, Olivia called as if right on cue. I told her about the hike and gave her the short version of my trip to Turkey.

"I think I'm losing my mind, Olivia. Any chance you could come for a visit?"

"I wish I could, but at this point Kevin doesn't seem to like it when we get together. Whenever I talk about it he gets upset. He thinks all this stuff is crazy. I am so sorry, Molly. I really don't want you to be alone right now. How long are you in town this time around?"

"I don't know yet, no word. Hopefully a little while. I need some time to absorb what is happening to me."

Then what she said about Kevin hit me like a solid punch in the stomach.

"Why would Kevin think like that? You and I have been friends our whole lives. You're my twin sister for God's sake! How long has he felt this way? Why haven't you talked to me about this?"

"It's not a big deal. Really. Nothing to worry about

at all. I'm sure he'll get over it. His Saturn is square his Pluto right now. He just really does not understand anything but hard science. Hopefully when his astrology changes later this year he will transform. Pluto is the transformer. I don't think you need a doctor at all. You're ready for a spiritual teacher or guide."

"When the student is ready the teacher arrives."

St. Anne's voice made me forget all about Kevin. Olivia heard her too.

"Listen to Anne, Molly. What about the gift certificate Penny Anne gave you? Why don't you call the psychic? Ask Penny Anne if she wants to get together with you tonight. I really don't want you to be alone."

"I have been alone most of my life, Olivia. Besides, there's a big storm coming tonight and I just want to light my fireplace and stay in. The volcano in Hawaii is going to erupt tonight and—"

"What? Molly, what are you saying?"

"I don't know what I'm saying. That's what I've been trying to explain to you. This is what has been happening. I guess the oracle is working on some level even if I'm not holding it or concentrating on it. Maybe you're right about the psychic. I'll dig up her number."

We got off the phone and I found the gift certificate sitting on my bedside table. Nothing was surprising at this point. It was actually just a sign to me that calling her was the right thing to do. I left a message on her voicemail.

The phone ringing startled me. It was the psychic's assistant calling back to tell me she had just had a cancellation so Stephanie could see me today at three p.m. Perfect. I had to leave shortly after she called to make it on time. Once again I saw the security guard in the parking lot, this time I waved. He waved back.

On my way to see Stephanie, Lisa called to apologize. Her husband had just called to tell her that his mother was dying of cancer. He suggested they start a family. Exactly as I had said.

"How did you know? He doesn't want to divorce. He said everything exactly as you said he would."

For some reason, I didn't feel comfortable sharing everything with her.

"Not sure. It just came out of my mouth."

"I'm so sorry, Molly. I want to be a better friend to you."

Time would tell.

As I made my way into the valley, I was excited but couldn't help but be a little nervous. I had never seen a psychic before. What was she going to be like? Would she use a crystal ball? Images flew through my mind. I would arrive to a neon PSYCHIC sign in front. They were all over Los Angeles.

I was lost in the daydream as I arrived at Stephanie's house. There was no neon sign. Instead, a beautiful well-kept cottage with white roses flanking the entry welcomed me. The smell of jasmine filled the air. I chuckled to myself. How silly our minds get when we are faced with the unknown. I took a deep breath and rang the bell.

Stephanie answered the door, greeting me with a warm smile. About my age, she was taller than me with long curly red hair pulled back in a ponytail. Her penetrating green eyes radiated love. It was immediately comforting just to be in her presence.

Inviting me inside, she asked me if I'd like a cup of tea as she showed me to a little guesthouse in the back with stained glass French doors. It was one big room with a loft she had remodeled to use as an office. She saw clients in the main room and kept a desk up in the loft. A large Warren Long oil painting of the Virgin Mary hung on the wall presiding over the space. A couch, coffee table and two chairs were the only furniture in the room. Sunlight poured in from skylights on the ceiling. Her office smelled like the same incense I had experienced at St. Ivar's on Christmas Eve.

She motioned for me to sit on the couch and sat across from me in one of the chairs. On the coffee table were a single white rose in a vase, a white candle which she lit as we sat down, a deck of cards and a framed piece of art 8"x10" or so propped up on an easel. The frame was draped with a crystal rosary. I felt the burning of my heart. Leaning in to see it more closely I realized it wasn't a normal piece of art. Inside the frame, there were six little roses. On top of each rose was a tiny piece of paper with writing that I couldn't make out, the ink had faded with age. An antique of some sort? It was too large to be what I thought it was—a relic.

"What is that?" I asked, pointing at the frame.

"It is a hair relic of St. Bernadette. The roses are made from locks of her hair. Are you familiar with relics?"

I just about fell off the couch. I certainly did not want to use my hour telling her about my secrets because I wanted to see what she knew.

"Yes. Yes, I am."

She smiled and her eyes twinkled.

"How can I serve you, Molly?"

"Well, I've never been to a psychic before. I'm not quite sure how this all works. Strange things have been happening to me and I feel like I need some guidance. Penny Anne gave me a gift certificate. She thought maybe you could help me."

She explained to me how she worked and how the session would go. She would begin with a prayer, and then she would do a reading using the cards for guidance. They looked a little like mine but were bigger and had different pictures on them. Tarot cards, she called them and they were wrapped in silk. She also spoke to the dead and could ask them questions. After the reading, if I had any unanswered questions, I could ask them then. She bowed her head and closed her eyes.

"Sweet angels of Molly Rose, use me as a conduit for your love and wisdom. Bring her the clarity and peace that she so desires."

She asked me to shuffle the cards. She then took the deck and began to lay out cards in the form of a cross. Stopping after ten cards she was very quiet for a moment, nodding her head as she looked at each of the cards. I was gripping the edge of my seat.

"You are a visionary, dear one. You are just coming in to your power. Many sacred things have been given to you and there are more to come. You have a man watching over you who is on the other side. 'Dad' he tells me. He says he loves you."

"My father," I whispered as tears welled up in my eyes.

"There are two men standing behind him holding large red crosses as shields. They are silent. He says you are doing everything right. Don't give up. He walks with you always. Does this make sense?"

"Yes."

Tears ran down my cheeks. I felt like a child. Stephanie handed me a tissue.

"With regard to the seven women, he says you already know some of them and you will meet the rest in your travels. Don't look for them. Let it all unfold. You must go to Greece. This is all he can tell you for now. He says he loves you."

"I love you too, Dad."

More tears followed by more tissues. Stephanie seemed to have an endless supply. I was obviously not the first person who'd been reduced to tears during a reading. I asked her about the purple cross but she did not seem to know how to answer. She went on to tell me that there was a very important man in my life whom I had already met. I mentioned Ankar and she confirmed he was my soul mate. We had lived many lifetimes together and I would be seeing him soon. She told me I'd be moving next year. Not clear on where, just that a move would happen. Lots of travel was in my future, but there would be a time of rest first. My relationship with my mom would continue to strengthen. There was a person I should be very careful with because they're not who they appear to be. She couldn't see who they were but felt it was a man.

"Someone very dear to you is going to leave your life. This is going to cause you much heartbreak but it is for the best and you will be able to see that one day."

"What do you mean, leave my life? Do you mean someone is going to die? My mom? Aunt Sally? I don't think I could take that right now."

"No. It will be like a death and you will grieve over it. It is part of a karmic agreement between you and this woman. More will reveal itself to you as time passes. Don't try to figure this all out with your mind, Molly. Use your heart to guide you. You have a very important mission to fulfill. You have specifically been chosen for it and must see it through. You are held and protected by a legion of angels, no harm will come to you. The Mother is with you every step of the way. It may seem as if your world is falling apart but trust me it is falling together. You will find great happiness. Our time is about out now, do you have any questions before I say a prayer to close the session?"

I asked if she could tell me anything about the location of the purple cross. She shook her head no, told me it would come to me and she bowed her head to pray. As I left she handed me a CD of the session. Thank goodness. Too much to remember.

"The truth goes into the bones."

As I was walking out to my car, Stephanie ran out with the relic and handed it to me.

"St. Bernadette wants to be with you now, Molly."

I hugged Stephanie, knowing I would see her again. Feeling the burning of my heart I got in my car feeling peaceful and content. Even the words she'd said about someone leaving my life didn't bother me. Something happened energetically while I was there, like I had been tuned or worked on in a way I couldn't see. My body was humming. Where was the purple cross?

The weather seemed to shift on the drive home. The sun disappeared behind ominous clouds. I arrived home just in time. Thunder rumbled as I parked my car. It was suddenly really cold outside. I lit a fire and made myself a frozen dinner. As I ate I reviewed the session with Stephanie trying to recall it, and discovered I couldn't remember most of it. I had the CD though and a new relic. I took St. Bernadette to my bedroom and introduced her to the rest of the girls.

The storm descended with wind and rain so strong that my windows rattled. Very unusual for Los Angeles. We hardly ever got rain and even when it did rain there was no thunder or lightning. It was strangely comforting to me. Maybe it reminded me of Idaho. As I watched the volcano erupt on the nightly news I suddenly felt wiped out and I fell asleep on the couch snuggled under a cozy blanket.

Ankar came to me in a dream. We were in my living room. It was completely dark except for a fire crackling in the fireplace. Naked, we stood facing one another. His eyes held the most profound expression. I could feel his love in every cell of my body. He wrapped his arms around me and it was electric. It absolutely took my breath away. He kissed me on the lips. My knees weakened. I couldn't stand up. He gently laid me on the couch exploring me with kisses, his hands caressing me in a way I had never been touched before. Each tender moment took me deeper and deeper into ecstasy. Starting at my abdomen, he began to drip honey on my body, licking it off as he made his way back up to my mouth. Then he kissed me, penetrating me at the same time. He tasted like honey. Oh my God. My body exploded from the inside out. Thunder erupted. My windows rattled. I jolted awake having an orgasm.

Slowly, I came back to the present. It was eerily quiet. I looked at the clock, eleven p.m. I stood up and saw stars. I thought I was going to pass out. My hands and feet were tingling. It is one of the wildest things that has ever happened to me in a dream to this day. I took a bath and prepared myself for bed. I was excited to go back to sleep. Maybe there would be more of Ankar. Just the thought of it made me blush as I crawled under the covers.

Unfortunately, it was impossible to fall asleep. Something didn't feel right. Sitting up, I turned on the light. A scene flashed through my mind—a clear vision. It was like watching TV. A huge fire was engulfing Laguna Beach. I saw it burning down many homes and I then suddenly saw Olivia's house on fire.

The vision passed quickly. I was left sitting up in bed, stunned. It wasn't a dream! I wasn't asleep. This was real and it just hadn't happened yet. I had to let Olivia know she was in danger. I dialed her, forgetting it was after midnight. Kevin answered the phone and said Olivia was asleep. I urged him to wake her up but he refused, asking what this was all about. I told him what I'd seen and warned him that they were in grave danger. I begged him to wake her up and evacuate as fast as they could.

The abrupt dial tone left me feeling helpless. I didn't know what else to do.

CHAPTER TWENTY-FIVE

Laguna Beach was burning. My phone rang at five a.m. Olivia, in total panic mode calling to tell me they were evacuating. We got cut off. I tried to call her back but all I got was a busy signal. I turned on the news. It was all happening, just like I saw in the vision. Horrified, I kept trying to get Olivia back on the phone but each time the busy signal blared in my ear. I sat down on the couch and took some long deep breaths. Then I prayed.

The shrill tone of the phone ringing made me jump. Olivia again. Thank God! She was in tears.

"There is no time—we've got to get out of here! Jason has got your things and just left. Can you meet him near Newport Beach? He'll text you where."

"Of course. I'll leave right now. No problem. I love you. Be safe."

"I love you too, Molly," she said sobbing.

I threw on some never-worn yoga clothes and flew to my car. I don't think I've ever moved so fast. Worried thoughts descended on me. Collecting myself, I prayed as I drove.

"Please help them get out safely. Please watch over them St. Anne."

"Be not faithless but believing."

Jason was waiting for me when I pulled up to our meeting place. The wind almost knocked me over when I got out of the car. The smell of smoke was thick in the air and it burned my throat. Jason looked grief-stricken as he put a small box on my front seat and hung the robe in the back. This was all a dream. He motioned for me to join him in his car and handed me an envelope. A note from Olivia:

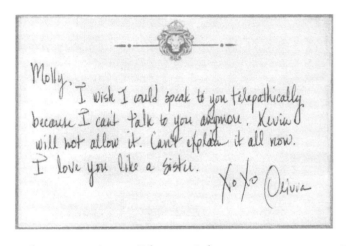

> Molly,
> I wish I could speak to you telepathically because I can't talk to you anymore. Kevin will not allow it. Can't explain it all now. I love you like a sister.
>
> XoXo Olivia

What? I tried to call her and there was no answer. I sent a text.

> Me: *What has happened? I do not understand. I love you. xoM*
> Olivia: *I love you. Kevin wants you out of our life. Nothing I can do.*

I looked at Jason. He wasn't just her chef, he had been her closest confidante during these years with Kevin.

"What does this mean?"

"It means you can not see Olivia again. Her livelihood is with Kevin and he is forbidding her to see or talk to you. She's a mess. Their arguments have been going on for a long time now. The fire has taken him over the edge. He's scared of you, Molly. He does not understand the power of spirit. He will find out one day I hope and then won't be so afraid of it all. Please know that Olivia does love you like a sister. We are trying to keep her as comfortable as possible."

He walked me back to my car and I lost it. Tears stung my cheeks in the smoky air. After he left I sat weeping in my car. Everything had burned away. I was standing in the ashes of a former life unsure how to move forward. For a moment I wanted to blame St. Anne but I knew she came to help not hurt me.

"Separation is an illusion."

I cried for over an hour, snot dripping down the front of my clothes, until I was spent. The sound of helicopters overhead brought me back to the present. I had to get out of here, away from the smoke. I looked at the box Jason had left on the front seat. I couldn't open it yet. My heart was cracked open.

The traffic was stop and go all the way back to West Hollywood. As I drove I thought about what Stephanie had said at my reading. Olivia must be the ending she told me about. I would never in a million years have imagined Olivia and I not being friends. It was just not an option. We had been best friends since childhood. There was nothing that could ever separate us. Yet, it had just happened. What was she thinking?

"Let go my dear."

Ok. I must. I must survive this. I thought about the note from Helena that had started all of this so many months ago. I had something important to do and I knew I could do it. I would focus on that, no matter what happened. It was everything. It was all I had left. Inhaling and exhaling slowly, I turned my thoughts to my mission. As soon as I shifted my thoughts I felt calmer. I had the relics of the seven saints as well as five of the holy objects that were clearly assisting me. I had no clue as to whom the other six women were who I was supposed to gather. I felt sure now that Olivia was not one of them. It had never occurred to me that she would not be one of them.

The robe was all I could carry when I got home. I had forgotten how heavy it was. I left the small box on the front seat deciding I would come back for it later. My apartment smelled like roses, but I didn't have any flowers there at all. The smell was so strong that I surrendered to the couch, closed my eyes and just breathed in the heavenly fragrance. Such a relief after the smoke. I heard to sit with my sacred objects. My heart burned. It wasn't Anne's voice this time. It came from deep within me.

Scooping up the robe I headed to my bedroom. There, on my altar was a picture of the Virgin Mary, the holy water from Turkey, Dad's photo and a photo of my mom and Aunt Sally as young girls.

I lit a white candle and placed it on the altar next to my relics. I picked up the key and added it to my St. Therese necklace, touching it with a sense of prayer. I thought of St. Anne and wished the relic was here with me now. It just didn't feel complete without her.

"I am with you always."

Standing in front of the altar with all my sacred objects gathered I put on the robe and moved into a trance-like state. Holding the oracle I closed my eyes and rapidly traveled back through time. Images flashed through my mind like a movie, different scenes or possibly lifetimes. Suddenly I was in a church. Latin words moved through my head, making their way to my mouth as I spoke them. A priest stood beside me waving a brass censer filling the church with the smell of incense. Holding a golden chalice in my left hand I pointed the first two fingers of my right hand to make the sign of benediction. The window with all its colors flooded me in holy light.

"Please help me, God," I whispered.

Suddenly, I was at the ocean, walking into it just as my father did. Oceana in all her glory was holding me and we were one. Then spinning... a flash of black nothingness...

"Oh no."

I managed to throw the robe off and fall back into bed. My body shook violently. It felt like a tidal wave of electricity was running through me. I was not strong enough to hold this. I had no control, but I was aware of everything that was happening.

"BREATHE!" my father's voice filled the entire room.

My body immediately reacted to his voice and I began to breathe in the way he'd taught me when I was a child. The breath lulled me to a deep tranquil sleep. I slept in the belly of the great Mother, hooked to her umbilical cord... immersed in light... weightless. Pure unconditional love. It was early afternoon when I finally woke up, groggy and disoriented. The robe was hanging on the doorway.

My chalice was one of the sacred objects that was missing.

When my doorbell rang I couldn't get out of bed because I was too weak. It rang a few more times. I couldn't move. Whoever it was gave up.

My body began to shake. Cold. Down to the bones. I needed a hot bath and fast. I sat in the tub and cried thinking about Olivia. The grief led me back to the loss of my father, which I had never really mourned. I cried until steam seemed to come from my heart. I actually saw it. Something shifted and I began to feel empowered. The feeling made its way throughout my body, fortifying me from head to toe. I knew I had to go to the ocean, to the great Mother. I had to make peace with Oceana for taking my father. I could do this.

I got dressed and put the oracle back in its swaddling cloth on the altar. Kneeling down, I removed St. Therese and the key from around my neck and placed them on top of the photo of my father. I prayed to my saints to protect and guide me. Oceana had called me.

My cell phone rang. My neighbor calling to let me know FedEx had left a couple of packages for me at her apartment.

"I'll be right over," I said and sprinted to her door.

She greeted me dressed in another one of my outfits from Olivia. I swear she really did do them justice. Holding up a small package she pointed to a larger one that she said was too heavy for her to carry. She did not want to ruin her nails. I easily picked up the box and she stacked the little one on top. Maybe because of the emotional rollercoaster I had been on all day, I'm not sure, but when I opened my door I started laughing and laughed until I almost wet my pants. She was too precious. She couldn't carry a box now because of her nails!

The small box was from Budapest. Inside, a beautiful card and message from Ankar, my heart skipped a beat every time I thought of him. And there wrapped in layers of tissue was St. Elizabeth. My heart burned. I felt blessed as I took the beautiful little relic to my altar.

I went to the kitchen to grab a knife to open the other box that looked like Fort Knox. It took me awhile to get through all of the packaging to a small black case with a brass handle. On top was a note that read: *For your sacred adventure. Mr. Philippe Dubois.*

It had a little lock on the front, but I pushed the button and it opened right up. Inside was an antique chalice. I lifted it out, awestruck. The lip was encrusted with amethysts and rubies and fine enamels of the Virgin Mary covered its base. I had called it forth and here it was.

I felt Oceana calling me again. The address my mom had given me for my uncle flashed in my mind. He lived in Malibu by the ocean. All this time I'd had his address but I had been too scared to go. Today was the day.

It was nearly sunset as I made my way up the coast. The box from Olivia sat on the front seat like an unwanted passenger. I was not ready to open it. Visiting my uncle's house was something I'd spent a lot of time thinking about. I had daydreams of him putting his arms around me, welcoming me home just like my dad would have.

From the street his house was nothing special. A small wood frame house full of windows with a deck that went right out on the beach. Warnings of a guard dog were posted on the wood gate that led to his house but I did not see or hear one. I parked up the street and walked out onto the beach. Peering into the house from the beach side, it appeared to be empty. There was a light on in the kitchen and I could see a white ceramic coffee cup on the counter. I moved back out onto the beach behind his house and sat down in the sand. The sun was beginning its descent in fiery crimson hues as I reflected on everything that had brought me to this moment.

With the exception of the purple cross, I had all of the sacred objects. As I had gathered each one and found the saints, I had been gathering myself. I healed my relationship with my mom. I did not know my father but I knew more about him than I ever had before. Now I had a starting point to learn more. My best friend had abandoned our friendship and my heart was heavy, but I felt stronger inside. I trusted myself now.

I thought of the saints who were with me and the virtues they represented. St. Anne had taught me the gift of humility. I gave her away to receive her. I learned that giving and receiving were the same. She was with me at all times. The boldness of St. Therese had come through Sister Violette who gave me the little flower. St. Therese, content with her humble life had given me permission to be content with mine. St. Elizabeth, the queen saint who gave generously all that she had. She taught me charity. I would always help others. The powerful St. Joan of Arc who was full of zeal gave me courage to fight for my mission, especially now after the fire. The Virgin Mary, our beautiful lady of grace taught me temperance. I must use moderation in my actions, my thoughts and my feelings. St. Catherine in her suffering taught me patience. She had such difficult circumstances but continued steadfast to share her visions. I would also share mine. The young St. Bernadette taught me chastity, to be moral and follow my personal guidelines of behavior towards others and to trust my own inner voice.

I had learned these traits and much about my own sins along the way. I knew I was strong enough now to overcome temptations. I was a woman now. Full of grace. I would be lead to the purple cross and then gather the women and do the ceremony. Nothing would stop me.

A young blonde angelic-looking boy walked by remarking that I should try out the water, "It's awesome, warmer than the air." He flashed a perfect smile and walked away.

Oceana called to me again. I put my feet in the water. Warm. I heard Dad teaching me, showing me how to hum. Voices beneath the hum repeated, "use your heart for good" over and over again. I moved my hands as if I had a basket in my grasp. My father had described the process in his journal when he wrote about the Hopi women. The waves slowed down.

I continued to hum, saying the words and moving my hands. The ocean became totally still. I walked out further as I hummed. The ocean heard me. The water was motionless. I moved out further and further. No fear. The ocean floor disappeared from beneath my feet. I felt like a mermaid. I could hear the other mermaids, singing, calling me to come out and join them.

Dogs barking on the beach behind me pulled me out of my peaceful immersion. Turning my head, I saw a large black man on my uncle's deck looking at me with scopes. The same man I had seen in my travels! Fear flooded me. I tried to keep my balance in the water, flailing my arms and legs about. My concentration lost, the ocean began to move again. Agitated waves pushed me forward and back.

Terrified and struggling to reclaim my focus, I watched the man make his way off the deck running across the beach towards me. He was yelling at me, but I couldn't make out the words. Something shiny was in his hand. It looked like a knife. Water slammed down over my head, filling my lungs. I was forced back up to the surface where I gasped for breath. The water took over; I had lost my control over the element.

"Lay your body back and float." My dad's voice filled my ears. "You are going to drown if you don't float. Let go, Molay. Stop resisting!"

The waves pulled me further away from the shore tossing me upside down. The undertow was pulling me out to sea. Oceana wanted me. I let go and stopped fighting. Something grabbed me underneath the water. My head hit a rock and everything went dark.

Floating up out of the water I saw the scene unfold below me. The black man pulled me to shore. Yes, *me*... I was watching myself down there. He laid something in the sand beside me and frantically gave me mouth-to-mouth resuscitation. The dogs continued to bark. I looked at the shiny object in the sand.

The purple cross.

"HELP!" he wailed.

"Molly. Molly, come back. You are a Rose. You are a Rose," he sobbed. "NO! Not again. Please God, not again!"

As the words left his lips the scene below me disappeared. Everything just disappeared.

~ The End ~

ACKNOWLEDGEMENTS

Thank you Joy for putting your heart and soul into this book, John for supporting me in all ways—you have a heart of gold, and to all of my friends who read, encouraged and assisted me: Katarina, Jana, Roger, Kara, Barb, Eliza, Kari, Stacy, Anna, Betty, Patricia, Julie, DC and Lori.

Thank you to the beautiful saints who guided me on this journey... especially St. Anne.

THE GIFT ~ READER'S GUIDE

Discussion Questions

1. The novel begins with Molly's dislike of Christmas and her loneliness. Do you experience the holidays in a similar way? Do you think of other people who may be alone during the holidays?

2. What are your thoughts about Molly's character? Has she become unhinged or crazy? Have you ever had a moment in your own life that utterly changed you or made you call into question your own sanity? When Molly is given the relic her life begins to change. Have you ever experienced a life change? Did you grow up with any religious influence?

3. There are several times in the book when Molly has to listen to St. Anne or an inner voice. Have you heard your inner voice and how would you describe it to someone else?

4. Molly gives St. Anne to her friend Olivia even though it has changed her life and given her so much pleasure. Have you ever given anything away that you truly loved?

5. Did you understand the concept of giving and receiving that Molly was learning in *The Gift*?

6. Molly has a dysfunctional relationship with her mother. Can you relate to wanting to know your parents in a real way? How did their healing feel to you? Do you think it changed Molly's life to really know her mother in a new way?

7. Molly quits her job without really knowing if a new job exists. This could be considered a foolish act. Have you ever taken this type of chance? Have you ever or do you currently work at a job you dislike? What would it take for you to jump out and take this kind of chance?

8. Molly was given her holy purpose. Is this something you are interested in? Do you feel you are here for something special? Can you relate to Molly Rose?

9. Penny Anne Saylor is always having a drink. Do you feel that much of your life is centered around alcohol or do you know people who require alcohol to socialize? How do you feel about that?

10. Molly is 38 years old when the book starts and not married. Do you feel that marriage is a societal demand? Do you feel that if you do not marry you do not belong? Did you feel pressure to marry and then have children?

11. The book is an easy read with a playful structure. Do you think it works?

Watch for Book 2 of the Molly Rose Series!

www.laurabushnell.com

14649262R00127

Made in the USA
Middletown, DE
07 October 2014